EAST
NASHVILLE
PRESS

HOPE

IS A

HARD

stories

THING

STACY DEAN CAMPBELL

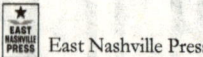 East Nashville Press

Library of Congress Control Number: 2026901200

ISBN 979-8-9943270-3-6

For Presley, Eva, and Ella

INTRODUCTION

Hope Is a Hard Thing is a collection of stories and ramblings I've picked up like souvenirs along the way. Some were carefully written, others were mined from notebooks, napkins, scraps of paper that followed me through ordinary days and long nights. Most of these pieces are fiction. A few lean close to memory. And some are just fragments. Unfinished thoughts that refused to be forgotten.

These stories live in quiet places. In kitchens after everyone has gone to bed. In towns you pass through and never quite leave. On empty train platforms and cheap motels off the interstate, in the sleepless grind of a truckstop. They belong to people carrying things they don't quite know how to put down yet, and to moments that arrive small but stay heavy.

I think hope runs through all of them, though not always in the way I expected it to. Sometimes it's stubborn. Sometimes it's fragile. Sometimes it's barely there at all. But it keeps showing up, again and again, in the spaces between what was lost and what might still be waiting.

This book is a collection of voices, places, and passing thoughts that together form a kind of record of trying, failing, leaving, staying, and learning how to live with the ache of wanting something more.

These are remnants of things I've carried around with me for a while. I hope you find something here that speaks to you.

Stacy Dean

CONTENTS

Mason   1

Yard Sale   7

Side By Side   12

Truckstop Candy   17

Run With Me   22

Hope Is A Hard Thing   23

Train Not Running   28

Company Man   33

Potash Miner   35

Palomino   36

Rio Grande   58

Redbird   59

Dirty Greyhound   62

Highway 90 West   66

Stagecoach 105   67

LaCaverna   74

The Sackman   76

Sugarboy   83

Thawing of a Reliable Man   89

MASON

THE RUSTY TAP had that Tuesday night quiet even though it was Saturday. Just the hum of the cooler and the bartender polishing a glass that didn't need polishing. Carl sat hunched over his beer, blazer still on from the funeral. A lapel pin from Harmony Lodge Chapter No.23, Free and Accepted Masons, caught the neon light and winked back at him in the mirror behind the bottles. He'd left the cemetery and just started driving, not thinking where. His car just seemed to turn itself here. He couldn't go home yet. Home meant his wife, Suzette, asking how it went and him saying, fine, when it wasn't. Home meant the TV blaring too loud and the world moving on like Leonard hadn't just died day before yesterday.

Carl sipped his beer. It tasted good and cold, the only thing all day that had done what it was supposed to do. Leonard had dropped dead taking out the trash. Heart. Probably the only thing about him that ever worked too hard. His wife, Barbara, found him just laying out there beside the trash can. Carl pictured her standing there in her robe, already planning how she'd tell it at church.

The door opened on three figures in dark sport coats. Gene came first, then Tommy and Earl, all of them with Harmony Lodge Chapter No.23 lapel pins. All of them tired and still carrying the weight of their own days.

"By god took ya'll long enough. Hell, I'm on my third already," Carl said.

"Shit," Gene said as he slid onto a stool next to Carl. "Doris wasn't even gonna let me back outta the house tonight. Had to slide up the garage door by hand and drive half way down the block with the lights off just to get off the street," Gene threw up a finger to the bartender.

"I didn't think Linda was even gonna let me go to the goddamn funeral this mornin'," Tommy added and slung up his hand too.

"I swear to god, I can't believe how scared you son's of bitches are of your own wives," Earl said and slid up on his own stool.

"Shit, you one to talk. You run your's off," Gene said.

"Hell, Suzette's scary as shit. I do whatever she by god says most of the time," Carl said.

They all laughed again and four frosty, cold beers appeared lined up on the bar in front of them. The bartender, who knew all of them by name, set out a bowl of peanuts and went back to pretending to polish.

"To Leonard," Gene said, raising his bottle.

"To Leonard," they echoed. The bottles clicked, a little bit like some holy offering if you didn't think too hard.

They drank long. Then sat in silence a moment.

Carl asked, "Y'all remember that camping trip he planned? The one where the tent blew into the lake?"

Earl laughed. "Yeah, and Barbara wouldn't let him go the next year. Said he wasn't responsible enough. Can you imagine? A grown man puttin' up with that kinda talk."

"Ol' Barb. I swear that woman," Gene said, shaking his head. "God love her, but she'd wear out a preacher."

"She'd wear out the Lord himself," Tommy said.

They laughed hard then, the big kind of laugh that feels

2

like oxygen after you've been underwater a minute too long.

Beers went down easy. Stories started to roll. Leonard's truck breaking down in front of the post office when he'd just run down there in his pajamas and house shoes to drop a letter in the slot. Leonard trying to fix his lawn mower with duct tape after Barbara threw a fit when he tried to buy a new one. Leonard sitting out in his garage in the dead of winter freezing his ass off just to be alone.

"He ever look happy to ya'll?" Earl asked.

"Once," Carl said. "Fishing down at the river. Had a cooler, a radio, no phone. Said it was the best day of his life. Then Barbara called 911 when he didn't come home by supper."

They all laughed again, but it was different this time, softer, with something heavy under it. Hours passed and empty bottles lined the counter like a crooked fence.

Gene wiped his mouth and said, "Boys, I been thinking." Carl groaned. "That's never good."

"No, hear me out now. You seen where they buried him, right? That double plot next to Barbara's?"

"Yeah," said Tommy. "He bought that back when he still thought love was permanent."

"He bought it back when Barbara still looked good," Earl added.

"Exactly," Gene said. "Now he's stuck next to her forever. That ain't right. You telling me that's where Leonard'd wanna be?"

Earl grinned, a mischievous light flickering in his eyes. "Probably rolling in that coffin right now trying to crawl away."

"Hell," Tommy said, "maybe we ought to help him out."

The bar went quiet. An idea hitting the air like smoke, thin and strange, but not completely crazy.

3

Carl rubbed his chin. "You serious?"

"Serious as a man can be with eight beers in him," Gene said. "And I can guar-an-damn-tee you Leonard would not want to spend eternity next to that woman."

Earl nodded slow. "Hell it'd be a kindness, really. A brotherly duty."

Carl took a long pull from his beer. "We'd be doing right by him. Wouldn't we?"

They looked at each other. No one said no.

A soft rain that had started to fall had turned to just a drizzle by the time they pulled into the cemetery. Earl's old Ford creaked under the weight of shovels, a cooler, and four bad decisions dressed in black suits.

Headlights swept across rows of stones, names catching in the light. They found Leonard's grave easy enough, fresh dirt and plastic flowers and a huge wreath from the lodge.

Carl stood there a moment with his hat off. "We sure about this?"

Gene cracked a beer. "Nope."

Earl handed him a shovel. "Then let's get to it."

It was real quiet, somber at first. Just the sound of metal in wet earth. Then someone started laughing. Tommy tripped over the cooler. Gene told a story about Leonard building a deck that collapsed under a grill and two cases of Coors. Laughter came easier after that.

They dug for what felt like hours, though it was probably less than one. The drizzle had stopped and a half-full moon had come out, watching like it didn't want to be part of this.

When they hit the top of the coffin, they all went still. Gene crouched, brushed the dirt away with his hands. "Hey, Leonard," he whispered, as if not to disturb any of the other dead lying around. "We're just moving you someplace better, buddy."

4

Then they pried the lid open a crack. That smell hit, sharp and real. They all took a step back, then laughed again, that nervous, stupid laugh that keeps men from admitting they're scared.

"Goddamn," Earl said. "He don't look half bad for a man that's been dead three days." "Shut it and lift," Carl said. They heaved the coffin up, grunting, slipping in the mud. It was quite a struggle, but they got it onto the truck bed, laid a tarp over it, and tied it down with bungee cords. Gene said it looked like they were hauling lumber. The dirt went back in much faster than it came out, looked like it had never even been disturbed.

"Where we taking him?" Tommy asked.
Carl didn't hesitate. "Down by the river."

The blacktop road gave way to dirt, then just ruts through weeds. They'd all fished here for years, before Barbara started calling Leonard home early for chores or some made up urgent matters.

Frogs croaked somewhere off in the trees, the river running dark and slow. They parked near the bank and turned off the headlights. Night folded in around them.

"Right here," Carl said, pointing to a rise overlooking the water. "This was his spot."

They set to work again. Dirt here was sandier, softer than at the cemetery. Moonlight made it look silver, pretty really.

For four drunk Masons in funeral clothes, they dug a respectable grave and eased the coffin down. Carl pulled off his jacket, wiped his face, and poured a little beer onto the mound. "For you, brother."

Gene and Tommy and Earl all took a turn to do the same and for a few minutes, nobody spoke. You could hear the river sliding by, calm and certain.

Gene finally said, "Ain't it something? A man's whole life, all his trouble, and it comes down to this."

Carl nodded. "At least now he's where he belongs."

"At least there's some peace in it," Tommy said.

"Least he don't have to listen to that goddamn hen-peckin' for the rest of all eternity," Earl added.

They stood around drinking what was left, telling more stories, laughing low, voices carrying just enough to sound like ghosts if anybody was listening.

When the beer was gone, they packed up and headed back. Earl's truck rattled over the bridge. Nobody said much.

Barbara came out just after sunrise, still in her house slippers, hair fixed, carrying a bouquet of carnations. Her knees ached as she knelt beside the headstone. She brushed some leaves away and straightened the wreath from the lodge.

"Leonard," she said, "I brought you fresh flowers. The others wilted already."

Her voice caught. "I wish you'd taken better care of yourself. I wish you'd listened more." She sighed and touched the stone. "You'd have liked the service. Carl and them came. You remember Carl. Always smelled like cigarettes."

She smiled a little then. "They were good to come."

Wind came low through the pines, just enough to move her hair. She thought it was a sign. She whispered something private and stood, brushed her knees off and walked away, slow and sure, back toward her car.

Down by the river, the water moved steady under the morning sun. Dirt piled in a mound on the hill was already settling. A fishing bobber, long faded and half-buried, rested near the grave.

Somewhere, a truck backfired in town. Day went on like it didn't know what the men had done, and maybe it didn't matter anyway. Leonard was where he wanted to be. And ol' Barb, bless her heart, would never know.

YARD SALE

HE WOKE before sunrise like always. Couldn't say why anymore, he just did. There was no job to get to. No boss. No reason at all except the rhythm of his old bones. The house was quiet. Had been for years. Just the refrigerator humming under the tick of an old wall clock.

The room sat stock-still in the half-dark, air a little stale as if it hadn't been moved around in days. He lay there for how long he didn't know, just staring at the ceiling. Light came soft through the curtains. That pale, sickly light right at dawn that can drag up mornings from fifty years back whether you want them or not.

He swung his legs over the side of the bed and sat up slow. His knees popped. His slippers waited on the floor.

When he clicked the light on in the bathroom, the mirror showed the truth. A face there that looked a little more gone than yesterday. Skin thin as tissue. Spotted up like dirty rain on a windshield. He reached for the razor and the shaving brush and went through the motions. Lather, scrape, rinse. A smell of soap filled the room, clean and simple.

He chose his brown suit from the closet. A little looser through the shoulders now, but it still fit. He worked the buttons through the vest, tugged the tie straight and set his old felt hat on his head till it felt right enough. Then he reached for the cane with the silver handle he'd brought back from France at twenty-three, back when his hands and his stride were steadier.

Before he left he stood in the doorway of the living room, looking around. The photos on the mantle were all there, his wife, the kids, him in uniform standing in front of a Jeep somewhere in the French countryside. He nodded once, as if to some old friend, then stepped out the back door and crossed the yard to the gate and went through and closed it behind him.

He tapped the cane on the sidewalk as he went along. He liked the sound of that, a solid little rhythm letting the world know he was still here.

He passed Mrs. Rollins' house with the pink shutters, then the old elm the kids used to climb, all of them hollering and flapping around and chattering loud as pesky, little magpies.

When he rounded the corner at Maple and Fourth, he saw a scattering of tables and cardboard boxes in a front yard. There were dresses on hangers, old tools, kitchen stuff, the kind of clutter that tells you a story's ending. A handwritten sign on poster board said YARD SALE in big blue letters.

He stopped and watched the women move about, folding things, rearranging. Something about the mess of it all pulled him in.

There were coffee mugs, picture frames, a box of records, a cracked lamp with a shade that might've been white once. He picked up a belt, worn smooth same as the one he used to wear to church. He gave a short, tired smile.

A ceramic rooster caught his eye. His wife used to have one just like it sitting on the kitchen window ledge.

Then he saw a small wooden box filled with old black-

and-white photos. He thumbed through them. People at picnics. Soldiers in uniforms. Kids on swings. None of them were familiar, but somehow they all were.

Something tightened up in his chest, the old homesick kind of tight that sneaks up on you when you're not looking, as he walked along, table to table, past a stack of folded quilts and a radio missing its knob. At the far end, near the shade of an oak tree, he saw a table covered in smaller knick-knacks. Jewelry, trinkets, keepsakes.

That's where he saw it.

A small silver compact engraved in a delicate floral scroll. He knew it instantly. His breath caught. His hand trembled as he picked it up.

He thumbed the latch and the lid clicked open. He didn't notice the cracked mirror, just the smell. Still alive somehow. Roses and powder, faint but sharp enough to cut through sixty years.

"Where did this come from?" he said out loud, but no one was near him. His voice sounded strange to his own ears. He looked around, heart pounding hard in his chest.

He traced the initials on the back with his thumb. M.R. Margaret Rose.

He closed his eyes, and there she was, standing on the platform in Marseilles with the sun dancing in her hair. She was laughing and holding that very compact in her hand, checking her lipstick. She'd looked at him and said, You'll come back for me, won't you? And he had come back. Married her under the cottonwood behind her parents' house. Fifty-three years of living, fighting, loving, and raising kids. Then gone.

He opened his eyes again and the present came back all at once, the tables, the strangers' voices, the smell of old cardboard and grass. He felt dizzy.

A woman's voice came from behind him. "Well hey there."

He turned, clutching the compact. The woman was middle-aged, hair pulled back, kind eyes, but he didn't really see her.

"Where did you get this?" he asked. His voice was hoarse, almost shaking.

She frowned a little. "That? Oh, that came from inside the house. We thought it might be worth a little something to the right somebody."

"Well, this don't belong to you," he said, louder now. "This ain't yours to sell. You hear me? This is...this is your..."

Something in her face froze him mid-sentence. The curve of her cheek. The small freckle near her eye.

He blinked hard. "I'll be damned if you don't look just like her."

The woman stepped closer now, "Dad," she said softly.

He stared at her, the world spinning beneath him. "What?"

"Dad, it's me," she said. "It's Mags."

He looked past her then, around at the tables again. The yard. The porch. The car in the driveway. The flowerbed with the little angel statue.

His yard. His porch and car and little angel statue. "Dad, it's Maggie."

He turned toward the house and saw the curtains he'd bought with Margaret thirty years ago, the ones she'd argued were too fancy but then said she loved. He turned back and stared a moment more.

"Magpie," he said quietly. "My Lord."

Maggie put a hand on his arm. "Dad, we told you to rest. We're just sorting some things before the movers come tomorrow. Remember? The nice, new place?"

He looked down at the compact again. His hands were shaking now. "You can't sell this. It's your mother's."

Her voice broke a little. "I know, Dad. Alright, we won't sell it. We just put it out by accident." She closed his hand around it. "Here. You keep it."

He nodded slowly, trying to swallow the lump in his throat. "She always kept it in her purse," he said. "Carried it everywhere."

"I know," Maggie whispered.

He looked at her for a long time. Same blue eyes, just older. "You got her smile didn't ya," he said.

"Come on, Dad. Let's go sit inside."

Before they went in, he turned again toward the tables, all the bits and pieces of a lifetime scattered in boxes and marked with prices written in black marker.

He thought of how things end up, a man's life broken down to twenty-five cent items under a tree.

Inside, Maggie helped him to his chair by the window. He set the compact on his knee and traced the engraving again with his thumb.

"How far'd I wander off this time?" he asked.

"Just around the block. You went out the back door again. You're not supposed to do that, remember? The stairs?" she said.

"Hell, I built those stairs. I can damn sure walk down 'em."

Outside, he could hear voices and laughter, someone haggling over a toaster. The sounds of life moving on.

He looked down at the compact again, the initials carved there by a young soldier with a pocketknife a lifetime ago.

Margaret Rose.

He smiled a little and whispered, "Still yours, darling."

The sun had climbed higher now, pouring through the

window, the silver throwing a hard little sparkle of sunlight across his hand. He sat there a long while, listening to the yard sale noise fade down to almost nothing, distance already doing its work.

SIDE BY SIDE

HE ALWAYS LEFT the office around five thirty if the day had been slow.

The days were always slow.

The elevator dumped him out into the lobby with the same dull thud every night. Outside, the cold crawled on the pavement looming like a predator. He pulled his collar up and walked to the platform at Clarke and Lake without looking at anything in particular. Was just the way he got through things now.

On the westbound L he slid into his seat by the window, the one he'd sat in so many times it felt shaped for his body. Frost filmed the glass. He wiped it clear with his sleeve until a square of the city came back. Blurred lights, old brick, a dirty slice of sky. He didn't peck at his phone. He didn't read the paper or a book. He just sat still. Waiting started somewhere behind his eyes before he even admitted to it.

The train slowed where it always slowed. Brakes hissing, metal grinding. They stopped on the elevated stretch above alleys packed with old snow and garbage bags split open by animals or somebody just hungry enough. Or both. Doors opened and he watched people pour in and out without making eye contact. Eye contact meant a possible conversation.

Nobody really wanted that. People just shuffled on and off, shoulders brushing.

Then eastbound train eased alongside them. He rubbed the glass clear again and saw her. Already seated.

Same window. Same coat buttoned all the way up, like she refused to let anything, even air, touch her skin.

For a minute she didn't look up. A minute that felt longer than it probably was. And when she finally raised her eyes looked at him, the ache he carried loosened. Not gone, just put somewhere he could live with it.

Neither smiled. Just held a look long enough to feel rude if it were anybody else.

Someone stepped between the cars. Then another. The space filled and emptied again. They were still there.

This was how it worked now.

At first it had just been recognition. Then expectation. Now it was ritual.

She began to notice when he was late. He noticed when she looked wrong. Tense. Withdrawn. Leaning into herself like she was bracing for something. Once, when his train pulled in and she wasn't there, his chest went hollow fast enough to scare him. Then she appeared at the last second, sliding into her seat, breathless and annoyed.

That night, she tapped the glass once with her knuckle. Not hard. Just enough.

He didn't respond right away. He just let the moment stretch a bit. Then he tapped back.

Then she smiled.

That stayed between them for weeks.

Different nights, different signals. If she leaned her head against the window, he knew she'd had a bad day. If he rubbed his eyes too long, she'd study him more closely. If one of them smiled and the other didn't answer it, the rest of the ride fell long and cold and flat.

Nothing ever passed between them that couldn't be denied.

At home, his marriage trudged on. His wife worked late. Or early. Sometimes she cooked. Sometimes she didn't. They talked about money. About the neighbor and his damn yapping dog that seemed to never sleep. They avoided the deeper things now. The meaningful things.

He stopped touching her for the most part, except by accident. She stopped touching him except through obligatory motions.

The woman on the eastbound train lived somewhere out past the places people chose on purpose. He knew that from the way she carried herself like someone used to waiting alone. He imagined her alone in her apartment Small and overheated, the windows painted shut. He imagined her, imaging him.

Some nights the trains stayed longer than usual.

One night it was snowing hard, flakes whipping, sticking to the windows like drapes. The platform emptied. Conductors leaned out and smoked. The doors stayed open, but no one moved.

She leaned forward and wiped her window clear this time, scraping the frost away with the edge of her glove until her face came into focus. He did the same on his side without thinking and for a second, they were framed perfectly. Side by side. Window to window. The rest of the world gone for a brief moment.

Her eyes dropped to his hands. Stayed there. When she looked back up, her mouth twisted into something trying not to smile.

He lifted his eyebrows. Barely. She shook her head once. Both laughed, that shy embarrassed kind of laugh that says everything and nothing all at the same time.

Another night, he realized she was watching him the whole time. Not looking away. Not apologizing. That kind of attention made his skin feel tight. Made his heart race. He shifted in his seat, then stopped. Let her see what she was seeing.

The next day he started wearing cleaner shirts. She started undoing one button on her coat. Small things. Stupid things. Everything said in silence.

Silence let each meaning stay flexible. Let it hover without dragging any consequence into it.

The night someone took his seat was the first time he broke that arrangement.

A broad-shouldered man stepped ahead of him and dropped down into his seat like nothing. The train stopped. Doors opened. The eastbound slid alongside.

He couldn't see her now.

He stood in the aisle, his heart thumping hard enough to make him feel dizzy. It surprised him how sharp and clear and fast the fear came up.

"Hey," he said. "My seat…"

"Find another one," the man said, without looking up.

He didn't think. Thinking would've stopped him. He pulled his wallet out anyway and peeled off a twenty.

For a second, holding it out, he felt exposed. Like he was tipping someone for letting him feel something.

"Take the bench," he said. "Please."

The man laughed and snatched away the money. Moved.

The window opened back up.

She had been watching everything.

Her reaction hit him harder than if she'd smiled. She didn't.

She studied him closely now. Her face serious. Somehow

18

curious. Then she lifted her hand, palm up, as if weighing something invisible. As if asking, Was that worth it?

He nodded. Once.

That seemed to satisfy her. She leaned back again. Looked tired then. Looked real.

After that, the air thickened.

Their looks lingered longer. Pauses stretched closer to action. When the trains pulled apart now, it felt abrupt. Jarring. Almost violent.

The last night he saw her, the delay was endless. Wind rocked the cars. Doors stayed open. Cold rushing in. But no one boarded. Everyone waited somewhere else. The city hissed and barked beneath them.

She pressed her forehead to the glass and closed her eyes. Without deciding to, he pressed in closer to his window. Mirrors of each other now, separated by grime and cold and laws of things not allowed.

Her eyes opened. Locked on his.

They stayed that way. Two people suspended. Not touching. Not leaving. Not pretending anymore. Until the doors closed and the trains yanked them apart.

The next night, her seat was taken by a teenager scrolling on his phone. The next night, no one at all.

He sat in the same seat without thinking. Wiped the glass clean. There was nothing there. He did it again the next night.

He always left the office at five-thirty when the days were slow

The days were always slow.

On the platform, a pause that once held something real now held only the idea of it.

He went home to his quiet marriage. The house was still and dark save for the stove light. Dinner plated and waiting

19

there for him. He ate by the light of the tv. Volume low
enough not to wake her.

TRUCKSTOP CANDY

THE MOON was just a sliver. The off-ramp dark as pitch, and her - a distorted silhouette carrying a beat-up guitar case - appearing out of the dark and taking shape in the glow of the sickly yellow truck lights that lay floating on a mist above the parking lot. She walked into the truckstop cafe and slid into a booth at the back of the dining room. It smelled in there. Stale cigarette smoke mixed with burnt coffee and cheap colognes and the faintest hint of the sweet acrid spices of bourbon and beer that collect in the skin and seep with the sweat. It was cold, temperature in the twenties at best, and she looked sheepish as the color began to return to her cheeks. In the light she looked to be no more than seventeen. As he approached the booth she pretended to be looking at the menu as if trying to decide what she might order to eat. He knew she wouldn't eat. They never ate. She closed the menu and said, "I guess I'm not all that hungry just yet. I'll just start with a cup of coffee and could you bring a lot of cream please."

When he came back with the coffee she was pecking at her phone and writing in a childish pink journal. She snapped the journal shut as he sat the cup and the handful of creamer down on the greasy tabletop. He watched her from behind the bar as she emptied the little plastic cups of creamer into the coffee and then turned up the sugar container and poured enough in to rot a tooth. She sipped the warm syrupy coffee and stared out the window across the parking lot into the murk of party row where sat lines of idling trucks, lurking in the dark.

That burnt coffee and old fryer grease and stale cigarette smoke drifted over the room, settling on her like a film. She wondered if she smelled like that now. She didn't want to smell like that. She shifted a little in the greasy booth, feeling the cold draft sneak under the window frame and crawl up her spine and she held the warm coffee cup with both hands, tight like she was afraid it might just decide to leave her too. Outside, a truck rolled by slow, its brakes whining, and she tracked it with her eyes, half-braced the way a stray dog watches a stranger. She wondered if the driver who'd dropped her off was still circling the lot somewhere, looking for another excuse to talk to her. He'd said she reminded him of someone he used to know. She figured was a lie men told when they wanted something but didn't know how to ask.

Her phone buzzed once, low battery warning, and she clicked it off. The black screen reflected her face back at her. She barely recognized herself in the neon light. She looked older, like months had been years.

She reached for her journal but she didn't open it. Just caressed the cover with her finger. Inside were things she used to want. Songs, mostly. Scraps of sentences. She wasn't sure anymore if keeping them meant she still had hope or if she just hadn't figured out how to throw them away.

Her step-daddy was from Michigan where he'd been an army recruiter in a strip mall. He had tattoos on his arms and across his shoulders and one, which she couldn't quite figure out what it was, below the belt line on his stomach. He said he'd seen a lot of action in the Persian Gulf, but she knew the only action he'd seen was in the Mediterranean restaurant in the strip mall. He was a purebred loser. She spotted it the first time he looked her up and down and said, "Well hello" in that stupid, creepy voice like he thought he was cute. He'd been relocated to Knoxville where he met, quickly moved in with and then married her mother. Her mother, who wore enough makeup to look desperate and enough perfume to smother out the gin. The first time, she fought like a cat in a bag. Scratching and kicking and biting. He did it anyway. After that she just figured the less she fought the quicker he'd be, and the quicker he'd be gone out of her room. Two weeks after her sweet sixteen, she made her way to I-40, stuck her thumb in the wind and headed west.

She dozed in the booth between refills of her coffee and watched the flow of truckers in and out of what they called the Trucker's Lounge. Black vinyl recliners and a TV hanging on the wall. And ashtrays. Lots of ashtrays. She knew there were showers back there, down the hall past the lounge. She watched them emerge like freshly shampooed dogs in flip flops and sandals. Overgrown baby feet, pink from the hot water in the shower stalls, parading into the adjoining convenience store; wandering the aisles searching for prepackaged sandwiches, chips, cookies, candy and pop to haul back to their lonely sleepers and cram into their round bulging stomachs.

He approached the table as she slept with her head resting on the windowsill of the booth. His voice startled her and she flinched and sat up wiping her mouth across her coat sleeve.

"Sorry, didn't mean to scare ya. I'm afraid we're gonna have to close up the dining room. Can I get you anything else?"

"Can I get one more refill on my coffee? It's really good and it's really cold tonight?" She laughed a nervous laugh and tried not to make eye contact with him.

"I'm afraid not. We've just poured out the last of it and started washing up the pots for tomorrow morning. Which ain't but about four hours now. The store part over there'll probably have some you can get 'fore you head out."

"Oh, yea, that's a good idea. I'll just get some over there. Do I pay you or somebody else?"

"It's just two dollars, you can just pay me right here."

"Oh, okay." She dug in her coat pocket and started dropping coins out onto the table.

"Say, I don't mean to pry, but is everything alright with you? Do you need me to call somebody to come out and pick you up? You been here a long time." He could tell the question flustered her and she looked for a moment like she might cry.

"Of course I'm alright. I just been sittin' here having some coffee and minding my own business. Is that not allowed? I ain't hurt nobody. 'sides, I got somebody I'm meetin' here later and we're going to Nashville, if it's any of your business. I'm gonna sing in a band over there. I thank you for your concern but I'm just fine." She dropped two dollars on the table and gave him a seventy-five cent tip.

She lingered around the front door and smoked Marlboro 100's in between attempts to pan handle a few dollars. He knew what she would do. What they all did as soon as they got cold enough. Cold. It seemed to be the fastest recipe for forty-dollar truckstop candy. She smoked the last of her cigarettes and watched her breath frost on the frigid night, pulled her coat up around her shoulders, picked up the guitar case and walked out across the parking lot toward party row. A big Navistar International with an oversized sleeper flashed its lights and she made her way over and climbed up into the cab. A lighted Coors beer sign hung on the front wall of the dining room with a small clock in its bottom left corner and a chain hanging down to switch the light. He stole glances at the hands on the clock as he swept and straightened the chairs and wiped the greasy booths. He felt queasy in his stomach as he watched the minutes tick by. After twenty, he watched her climb down out of the cab straightening her clothes. A Freightliner three spaces up flashed its lights and she walked to the big truck, stepped up on the running board and tapped on the passenger side door. The door opened and she climbed up and disappeared into the darkness.

He sat there staring out the window for how long he didn't know. Thinking about what he could do. Knowing he couldn't really do anything. He'd seen plenty of girls like her before. Running in thin coats, tired eyes, that jittery way they looked at doors. He never knew what to say to them. Never knew how to help without making it worse. So he just carried the weight of it home and set it down beside all the other things he couldn't fix. He stood to go, glanced back once more at all the idling trucks lurking there in the dark. Then he reached and pulled the chain and the Coors sign flickered out. He went out the back door and locked it behind him.

RUN WITH ME

TRUCKSTOP DINER 1 a.m. I watched a man sitting at the counter drinking coffee. Cup after cup of stale, black coffee. Watched as he avoided eye contact with the waitress, a Mexican woman weathered but very pretty. All he ever said to her was thank you. He started to try and make conversation with her a time or two but stalled. After a while he stood to go. Left his money on the counter and headed for the door. He stopped and looked back. She caught a glimpse of him watching her and smiled warmly, then continued down the counter filling coffee cups. The little bell on the door clanked as he left. She stood and watched his taillights disappear up the on ramp. Don't know why he didn't talk to her. I would have talked to her.

HOPE IS A HARD THING

THEY INSISTED on calling her Miss Lenore. She hadn't been "Miss" anything in decades. She didn't care for it, but she wasn't the wandering kind. Didn't get confused, didn't get loud. And they let her live in Room 110, close to the nurses' station and she liked that. So she didn't complain. Just stayed quiet in the way worn-down people get quiet. Worn down to where it feels like every word costs something you just don't have a whole lot of left anymore.

Sometimes the nurses wondered what her voice had sounded like before the quiet set in. They way her eyes still darted, quick as minnows in a bucket. You get old and one of two things happens, you soften up or you get carved down to the bone of who you've been the whole time. Lenore looked carved down. Looked like someone who'd spent her whole life tying together loose ends while the world tried its damnedest to pull them apart.

She came to Landsun after a bad fall in her kitchen. Broke something that didn't heal right. Rehab that didn't fix much. Her daughter brought her in wearing sunglasses inside the building. The staff remembered the perfume more than the face.

Lenore watched her go and didn't say a word. Just held her purse tight until the shaking in her hands settled.

After that, she waited.

Room 110 had a view of the river if you tilted your head just right and the weather was clear. It wasn't a real pretty river. Water moving slow, the color of old pennies. Not the kind of river that makes for postcards, but it moved, and that was something.

On good mornings the sun hit the glass and turned the water the color of weak tea. Reminded her of the kind her mother used to make. Sun-brewed with lemon and enough sugar to make a spoon stand straight up. She'd lean in close to the window and pretend she could smell it again. The windows didn't open, though. All she really smelled was a hint of PineSol from the night crew.

She'd sit wrapped in a pilled blanket donated by the Methodist ladies and watch the cars pass by. Every time a phone rang down the hall, she straightened a little.

"She's coming," she'd say. "My daughter said she'd come this weekend."

She said that most weekends.

Sometimes she'd talk about her daughter. Not stories, exactly, more like scraps. A doll she begged for one Christmas. A dress she wore till it frayed. A laugh that used to fill a whole room. Things Lenore carried like shiny coins in her pocket worn smooth from her thumb rubbing them.

She never talked about the later years. The quiet ones. The drifting ones. It felt like there was a whole other story there but she kept that one for herself.

Nurses rotated shifts. Young ones with tired eyes, older ones with smoker's coughs that rattled like loose engines rods. They weren't unkind. They just learned everybody's patterns.

Lenore's pattern was waiting.

Waiting turned into the shape of her days. Began to

identify her like a job. Some people wait angry. Some wait scared. Lenore waited with the worst kind: hope.

Every time a car slowed outside, she lifted her chin. Every time footsteps came down the hall, she breathed shallow and listened. Every time they passed her by, she blinked it away like dust in her eyes.

"You want to play bingo tonight?" they'd ask.

"Better not," she'd say. "Might miss her."

"Want some birthday cake down in the dining room?"

"You go on. I'm fine here."

She wasn't fine. But she said it like someone who'd long ago accepted that fine wasn't coming back.

Some nights she lay awake staring at the ceiling tiles. Whispered to herself, practicing hellos nobody else heard.

Loneliness is quiet until it isn't. It sits in a chair beside you, settles in your bones. She'd think about her husband, who used to whistle walking through the door after work. Think about her sisters, all gone now. Think about the daughter who still lived somewhere on her map of hope, though that map was shrinking down to almost nothing.

She wasn't crazy. Just old in the way where people drift off and no one tells you what to do, how to live after their gone.

For weeks something had been settling inside her. Not sadness exactly, more like a decision.

The morning she left, frost dusted the windows, the whole place look dipped in sugar. The world felt brittle.

Lenore woke early and moved slow but sure. She washed her face in water so cold it shocked her breath out for a second. Hands gripping the sink until everything steadied.

She fixed her hair the way her mother had taught her so many years ago. Comb smoothing the top, sides pulled back neat, ends tucked behind her ears. It had been years since she'd bothered. She didn't look younger, just more like herself than she had in a long time.

She put on cheap red lipstick, the shade her daughter said made her look "a little too much." That made her grin. Life had never given her much, so she swiped on a bit more.

From the bottom drawer of her dresser she took out her good navy dress and pulled it over her head and smoothed it across her legs and eased the drawer shut like the sound itself might wake a ghost.

Her hands only shook once, when she clasped the necklace her husband gave her for their tenth anniversary. The clasp was stiff, but she got it.

She didn't take anything else.

The night nurse was scrolling on her phone. She never even looked up. Old people wandered around sometimes. Nothing unusual.

The front doors slid open, and the cold rushed. Lenore didn't flinch. Just stepped out and let the doors slide closed behind her.

Nobody saw her cross the road. Nobody saw her make her way down the ditch, careful and determined. The sun was barely coming up, sky the color of burnt copper.

The river was only thirty-odd yards off the parking lot. The administrator once said they ought to put up a fence. They never did, and nobody argued.

She reached the embankment. Mud sucked at her shoes as she climbed down. She stumbled once but caught herself on a branch.

The water came up cold and fast. Past her ankles. Then her knees, her waist. She gasped once at the shock but kept walking.

She stepped into that river like she was going home. Stepping into her own kitchen, quiet and sure. No hesitation.

Just a long breath and then letting go.

The current took her legs first. She didn't fight. Just closed her eyes.

The river hummed, low and uncaring. It didn't judge her. Just moved along, the way it always had.

Then she was gone.

Her coat snagged on branches near the bank a few hundred yards down river. A groundskeeper found her around eight-thirty and called it in with a voice that shook a little. Deputies came quick, lights flashing, sirens barking.

They pulled her out with an extra dose of care. Covered her face. One deputy cussed under his breath soft, like some sort of half prayer.

"She went on her own," another said. "This wasn't just wandering off."

A nurse cried until her mascara ran down her cheeks.

They finally reached her daughter on the third call. She was at work, background clatter, music, everything too loud for this kind of call.

"What?" she said. "Oh my God. What happened?"

"She left the building," the nurse said.

"What do you mean left? She can't just…"

"She just walked out," the nurse said. "We think she might have been looking for something."

A long silence.

"I meant to visit," her daughter said, voice breaking. "I really did."

"She knew," the nurse said, lying the way people lie in those moments when the truth is just too much.

The service was two days later in the little chapel. No flowers except the fake ones. A Bluetooth speaker crackling out a hymn.

The maintenance man stood in the back with his cap in

his hands, sniffling like he had a cold.

The daughter talked about peace. Someone else talked about rivers and rest. None of it sat quite right.

Afterward, one of the nurses walked down to the water. Watched the current roll on, steady and indifferent.

"She deserved better," the nurse whispered.

The river held no judgment. It just kept moving. Like it always had.

TRAIN NOT RUNNING

IT WAS still dark when he rose and picked up his boots from beside the bed and shuffled down the hall in his bare feet toward the kitchen. She stirred and rolled onto her side, but didn't wake. When the room went still again, her breathing slow and rhythmic, he picked up his boots from the side of the bed and shuffled down the hall in his sock feet toward the kitchen. He knew every creaky floorboard in the hallway by heart and he knew what a light sleeper she was and he navigated the ancient planks on tip toes past the frozen faces of long-departed kin, yellowed behind their glassed frames, watching him until he stepped onto the linoleum in the kitchen.

He stood at the stove and watched the coiled burner redden and come alive like a stir viper, its heat drifting upward and flushing his cheeks. Coffee perked. The scent of it made his mouth water. He poured a cup and sat and listened to a nightbird calling somewhere in the dark and stared hypnotized into the blackness of his cup.

The big white house sat no more than twenty yards from the train track. At the edge of the yard the earth sloped up to the rails that had lain there long before he was born. The yard so shallow, had a passing train ever jumped the track, it would have topple the back porch and part of the kitchen. He finished his coffee, rinsed the cup, and set it upside down on a towel. He took a burlap potato sack from a drawer and stuffed it in his back pocket where it hung down like the frayed tail of a squirrel. The sun had begun to cast faint shadow as he stepped out and clawed his way up the slope onto the railroad track.

Hollis lit a cigarette and sucked the menthol into his lungs. Tracks ran overgrown as far as he could see. He walked past rotting trailers, sinking houses, garments hanging on clotheslines swaying in the breeze like odd dancers. A wiry pitbull with a head wide as a cooper's anvil charged full speed up the slope but jerked back at the end of its chain. He leaned forward, just out of reach, and spit on the dog's forehead as it choked and fought the pull.

"Dumbass. It's just gonna do the same damn thing every mornin'," Hollis said.

He continued down the tracks another mile and stepped onto a faint trail ascending into the dense growth of Little Black Mountain.

Near the top, a sagging barbed-wire fence crossed the trail. A faded no trespassing sign hung from the top wire. Fence posts leaned like dozing guards. Hollis caught his breath, then stepped through and listened. A Brown Creeper called from high above, matched by a Mockingbird until an unseen owl hooted and silenced both. Sunlight broke over the treetops and amber shafts pierced the foliage, stirring the forest floor. Small creatures rustled, fleeing the sudden light.

Convinced he was alone, Hollis moved up the trail another fifty yards, then pushed into the undergrowth, eyes scanning the ground. Ginseng was hard to spot unless in bloom. In bloom, the red berries shone like tiny bursts of neon. Out of bloom, the leaves could fool an untrained eye into thinking poison ivy.

The first plant grew beside a downed tree. He listened again, then opened his pocketknife and crouched to work, cutting away the leaves and digging at the earth. He freed a long, twisted root that looked like the dirty hand of a small witch. He brushed it clean, inspected it, dropped it into the net sack, and continued across the hillside.

Produce in cardboard boxes lined the tailgate of Jay Boy Patterson's old Ford: sweet corn in pale husks, okra pods, and tomatoes buzzing with flies. Jay Boy sat in a folding chair beside the hanging produce scale. He leaned back as Hollis approached.

"Where'd you get these roots?" Jay Boy said as Hollis dropped the sack beside him.

"What?"

"You heard me."

"Well, I got 'em from the gettin' place. What in hell you care where I's to get 'em from?"

"'Cause they ain't dickin' around no more that's what. These come off'a private property, I might be up shit creek. Folks gettin' shot for trespassin' now. It ain't like it used to be."

"Hell they's roots, Jay Boy. You think they got microchips or serial numbers in 'em? You want 'em or don't you?" Hollis said, reaching for the sack.

"Hang on now. I ain't said I didn't want 'em. Just ast where they come from."

"Well, they come from over yonder. Now weigh 'em and pay me out so's I can go on."

Jay Boy poured the roots into the scale. The needle danced before settling a little over fifteen pounds.

"Heard Westmoreland gonna go at Bonny Blue again," Jay Boy said.

"Hell you say. Train ain't run near Bonny Blue since I don't know when."

"They say some new geologist found seams that got missed."

"Blue Diamond nor Westmoreland neither one ever missed a damn thing," Hollis said. "If they's seams left, they missed 'em on purpose."

"Well, I'm just sayin'. I'll go two and a quarter."

"You a crook, Jay Boy. You know it. Go on and give it here."

Hollis counted the cash and headed home through town. The place looked apocolyptic. Deserted if you didn't know better. He passed the Christ Church with its peeling trim and an old company store with broken windows and a sagging porch littered with beer cans. The hills were dotted with shacks scattered like trash thrown from a car. Rows of abandoned coal-company houses once full of miners now sat silent.

He felt watched, paraded past the eyes of ancestors he only knew from half-drunken stories told by his father and grandfather. Stories of wages, strikes, black lung, and pride. He was cut from that cloth. Coal ran in him same as it had in them. He was a coal miner whether the train ran or not.

A strange energy crept into his step. Once he recognized it, he cursed it and crushed it down. He stopped in front of a dirt-covered window where a looter had wiped a small clear patch. In the glass he saw an old man in a young man's clothes staring back. He lit a cigarette, picked up a golf-ball-sized rock, and hurled it. His reflection shattered and fell into the overgrown grass.

Time had a habit of crawling into beer cans at the Bobcat Den. Many a man had lost hours in its cool jukebox hum. It was after nine when Hollis stepped outside and crossed the gravel lot onto the tracks. In the black night, all of him disappeared except the glow of his cigarette.

The house was dark when he came in. He moved quietly into their bedroom and laid the rolled money on the dresser by her side. He washed his hands and face, dirty water dripping into the sink.

She stirred and opened her eyes as he crossed the room and stood silhouetted at the window, looking down at the tracks.

"Hon," she said.

"Yea."

"You know whatever they're doin'back up in there, it ain't gonna last."

"Hell, I know. But for a minute, I can dream, cain't I?"

He watched the rails glisten in the moonlight a while. Then he unlaced his boots, set them beside the bed, and slid under the sheets. She pressed up against his back, her breath warm on his neck.

"Love you," she whispered.

"I know."

That night the first of thirty coal cars backed under the loader at Bonny Blue Tipple. A screeching, grinding wail tore through the hollow. He opened the window as the train crawled past. The howl of the big Norfolk Southern engine rattled the walls. And for the first time in a long while, he slept the sleep of the dead.

COMPANY MAN

NOT SURE if you're asleep or not. You asleep? Don't know what started that fire. Didn't nobody really say for sure. Said it might've been some jackass trying to smoke a cigarette. You know, they say there's pockets of gas hanging low all over those shafts. You can't smell or see or nothin'. Wouldn't have no idea what was hanging all around your pant legs. It's heavier than air, you know? W'y in hell would you chance somethin' like that knowin' it could blow you and everybody else to kingdom come? I just can't figure it. Can you hear that night bird cawing? Big ol' black crow. Sounds like he's sittin' right on the sill. Been there for I don't know how many nights now. I just can't sleep with him cawing all night long like that. Anaconda's as good a company as any. Always treated me fair enough. Hell, I didn't have not a thing in the world to do with any of it. Not a damn thing and would you believe Ira Whitaker's widow spit on me today. Walked right up to me and spit on my fresh shirt. I didn't know what to make of it. I didn't have a thing in the world to do with any of it and she spit on me like I's the one what caused Ira to get killed. I liked Ira. Hell, I felt plumb sick when they said he's among the ones burned up. I just stood there and didn't say nothin'. I'm just a bookkeeper for Christ's sake. I just keep the ledgers balanced. That's it. I've never even stepped foot in that mine. Anaconda's an alright company. It's a job. Well, I got the baby's milk anyhow. You know those little condensed cans that she drinks so good. And I'm sorry, but I don't think you and the widow Whitaker are still much good friends. I know you always thought a lot of her, but I was hoping you might understand. There's just no other jobs around here for somebody like me. No other company big enough to need a bookkeeper full time. Numbers are a talent you know. I'm sure if Ira or any of the rest of them had've known how to balance books, they would've been up in the office right alongside me. You can't spite a man for using his talent to tend to his family can you? Can you? I know you're ashamed. You say you're not, but I see it. I feel it when we're in town. Well, I'm not ashamed. Said it was supposed to get down near twenty degrees the next couple nights and you and the baby are warm. Why should I be ashamed? I didn't have nothin' to with it. Why should I bare any of the guilt? I just keep the ledgers balanced. I don't know if you're asleep or not. Are you asleep? How can you sleep with that damn bird cawing all night long?

POTASH MINER

MY GRANDFATHER was a potash miner. As you probably don't know what potash is, you can guess that he didn't much either and became a miner of this ore by chance and not by choice. Six farmless farmers loaded in a car, three across the front seat and three across the back, pulled onto the highway and started out toward California. No honest work left in Arkansas. Going to pick peaches, oranges, apples, cherries. Anything that needed picking. Stopped for gas in Carlsbad, New Mexico. Saw a notice for men wanted at Duvall Potash Mine. The other five went to California, he stayed right there. Mined potash for forty years, raised five children, died, left each one of his kids a little money, and lays in a plot in the desert next to his wife. Always hated the dust and the desert and never stopped wanting to go back home to Arkansas. He never even could quite tell me just exactly what potash was. Last time I asked him what he dreamed of he said, "A good team of buckskin mules, a plow, and a little land to churn up. I just love to drive a good team of John mules."

PALOMINO

THE MEXICAN stood barely five feet three inches tall in his boot heels. He sat atop a worn black saddle with loud silver conchos on each side of the saddle horn that flicked a glint of white-hot light popping and ricocheting off every surface he passed. His pants and shirt were thin and weathered, with sharp metallic creases that the fabric was just dense enough to hold. He wore a Silver-belly hat dusted with a powder of silt revealed in a dark ring of sweat, contrasting it against the similar color of the felt. His boots also collected the fine dust, indicating a ride of some distance down an unpaved road before clip clopping onto the main thoroughfare of the border town. The Palomino was a big Tennessee Walker gelding with a slick straw-colored coat, mane, and tail and four creamy white socks that could have been painted on with the same even stroke six inches above each hoof. He was a big horse that reached eighteen hands if he reached one and the pair looked peculiar in their mismatched proportions. There was a nobility about the Mexican, a confidence of place and valiance, like a small child riding a pony round and round a hot walker in a parking lot carnival. As they strode down the street past the café, and then the drugstore, the big horse obeyed the slight-est flick of the reins moving in absolute synchronization with his rider as he came to a stop at the light post in front of the Regar Agujero bar. The Mexican dismounted, tied off the big Palomino, and looked around proudly, searching for some adoration, some manifestation of envy. Melancholy blew through the parched town on a loose page of the Grit newspaper, floating softly past the Regar Agujero and catching in a chain-link fence where it waved like a tattered flag over a land conflicted between dwelling and desolation. A scrawny dog darted in and out of the shade exchanging yaps with the gruff barks of a larger dog somewhere in the distance. One old man sat on a bench across the street and snored and startled himself awake, blinking blurry incoherent eyes at the Mexican and his fine horse before letting his fleshy chin slump and continue its cadenced rising and sinking against the heave of his chest. The Mexican's scrunched brow and slumped shoulders revealed a vague disappointment in that there was to be no fanfare on this, or any other day, for a proud vaquero parading an impractical Palomino down a mid-afternoon street in a border town in Texas.

Parked in front of the Regar Agujero sat a monstrous robin's-egg blue Buick. The Mexican almost walked right past it. He was so entranced by the thought of the icy cold beer nestled deep in the cooler behind the bar, he almost hadn't noticed the out of place automobile. The type of automobile he had only seen in newspaper pages the barber would put down around the base of his pneumatic chair to catch the clippings of falling hair. The barber was thought by the Mexican to be a lazy man who did not tolerate the heat well and felt that the more hair the paper caught, the less sweeping he would have to do. He had even on occasion asked the

Mexican to pick up the paper of his own hair clippings and toss it in the trash out back before he left. More than once the Mexican had brushed away the clippings of his hair and stopped to admire the new models of automobiles in the advertisements before he threw the paper away. Now and again he would give in to his nature and allow himself to struggle there in the alley with the pangs of longing for the prosperity that had always eluded him, and the realities behind his façade of complacency. Knowing it would be at least two lifetimes before he could ever hope to acquire enough for such extravagance, he would crumple the paper and mutter to himself in the maundering tongue of the poor who try to convince themselves that wealth is foolishness and wouldn't be had on a dare.

He stood pondering the car a moment, then stooped and peered inside, his hat bumping the window like the beak of a confused bird flown into a house and trapped behind a glass. Tilting his hat back on his head he pushed his face close enough to escape the sun's glare and his nose pressed three small greasy smears on the glass as he surveyed the car's interior. Loud promising Las Vegas pamphlets lay strewn across the front seat and spilled onto the floorboard. Cigarette butts, stained with deep red lipstick, bled out of the ashtray, gnarled like severed fingers crammed to capacity in the hole in the middle of the dash. Suitcases in various shapes and sizes lay across the back seat; a masonry of alligator print bricks stacked almost to the headliner. As he turned and walked toward the door he caressed the fine silt on the front fender, gentle and deliberate as if wiping powder from a woman's thigh.

The Mexican paused in the open doorway just long enough to remove his hat and adjust his eyes to the dusty light of the little barroom.

"Comos se cuelgan pequeño vaquero?"

The familiar voice came from somewhere in the hazy abyss and the Mexican answered back projecting his own voice in the general direction of the comment, his squinting eyes and head searching the room as with the conversings of a blind man.

"Al igual que un molesto tercera pata mi amigo, como una tercera pata."

The bartender roared a bellowing laugh that rattled the entire little bar deep into its structure and popped a thick sweating bottle of beer down in front of the Mexican as he climbed to his usual perch atop one of many tattered barstools.

"¿Quiénes son los gringos?" the Mexican said to the bartender as he thumbed at the two out of place gringos in the corner.

"I don't know. They've been in here all morning. They are paying for their beers in advance though, so I don't care who they are. I hope they sit there all day."

The bartender was a short round man who wore his hair combed straight down in a hard bang, stuck against his forehead with a gummy sheen of hair tonic. Above his lip grew a thick black mustache that he proudly named Pancho Villa and spoke to, often insisting to patrons that it had the supernatural ability to predict various stages of the human condition. He had acquired the Regar Agujero from his brother, who had deeded it to him in an attempt to keep it from his malevolent sister-in-law, who had announced her intention to divorce his brother and take "everything that sorry bastard had ever thought about owning" with her. The Regar was deeded to the bartender for the sum of one dollar to keep things legal and the promise that he would sell it back to his brother for two dollars once the brother's divorce was final. The bartender refused and retained ownership of the near dilapidated establishment, the brother having never stepped foot in it, nor spoken to him, since.

The Regar Agujero was a small clapboard building with a concrete porch running its width. Every surface inside was covered. A tapestry of current and past events, near brushes with fame, and ancient headlines, yellowed and tattered from having been unreplaced for decades by any new happenings in the sleepy town worthy of a clipping. Bottles of amber liquors lined a shelf behind the bar, which sagged in the middle and bounced slightly upward when relieved of the weight of one of its poisons, momentarily removed at the behest of a patron. A metal fan hummed a whining monotone and stirred warm air across the floor as a small transistor radio crackled western music out of San Antonio. A few regulars sat scattered around like dusty fixtures permanently attached to their perches, camouflaged in the dingy monochrome of the room. In the corner closest to the door, at a table flooded with gold light from a dingy bulb that reflected the nicotine-stained underbelly of its ancient tin shade, a gringo man and gringo woman huddled close to each other, sipping their warm beer and giggling. The gringo man was small and doughy with the plump pink face of a child. His hair neatly combed in a hard part and squeaky clean. He wore starched gabardine trousers with a cuff short enough to reveal nylon stocking socks that covered his dainty ankles. From his shirt-sleeves hung two sun-scorched arms lacking definition.

His feet sheathed in glossy leather loafers tapped nervously at the floor. A perfectly proportioned man in miniature, propped up, posture perfect at the table admiring his prize. His prize, a well-built redhead from Austin. She'd met her little man while she was waiting tables in a bar in the lobby of the Driskell Hotel. She had gotten the job while wearing a dress with no stockings underneath, revealing her long bare legs, and heels with a strap around the ankle and open toes revealing her bright red toenails. The manager had taken one gawking look up and down her perfectly proportioned physique, fixed his eyes on her heaving bosom, and immediately told her she could start her new job that very evening. She was well versed in using her allure to her advantage.

Flies buzzing. Fan swirling. The Mexican took a long gulp of his beer and wiped his mouth on his sleeve.

"I guess that's his car, no?"

"What? Do you think I had some rich uncle to go and die and leave me a car like that or sontheen? Whose else would it be? Of course it's his car," the bartender said, flailing his hands at the air.

"Aw, si, si."

Studying the gringo man in the mirror over the bartender's shoulder, the Mexican said, "What do you think he does?"

"I think he drives a nice car," said the bartender, leaning in toward the Mexican and lowering his voice, "and prob'ly gets to see her naked."

"Eh, probably. Imagino que."

"I can't. I can't imagine sontheen like that, I might pass out and fall and hit my head on the bar. Then while I'm knocked out you would drink up all the rest of my beer for free."

"Well, try real hard to imagine it then," said the Mexican, "all that creamy white skin."

"Stop it. Now I'm not kidding. Stop it and I'll give you one on the house. If you just shut your mouth, usted pervertido."

"Pervert? You started it. 'sides, they're probably married and he's bored as hell. And she's probably a protestant."

"Eh, maybe. But he don't look bored to me."

From the corner came a warm rumble of drunken laughter and the Mexican and the bartender turned and watched the gringo woman stand and stroll across the room and disappear into a bright light that exploded like burning phosphorous into the bar as she opened the door. Within moments she burst back into the room and skipped back over to the table where she grabbed the gringo man's hand and pulled at him, urging him toward the door. His momentary resistances and whinings were futile. He was dragged along behind her like a delinquent schoolboy. Head down, feet shuffling, shoulders dropped out the front door. Within a few moments the door exploded open again to a dull rolling grumble across the room. The woman returned to her seat at the table and sipped her beer and lit a cigarette letting smoke billow out of her red pursed lips and float softly around in the gold light. The man stood and surveyed the room and then walked over to the bar.

"Excuse me, would you happen to know whose horse is tied to the post outside?" the gringo man asked.

The bartender glanced at the gringo and gave a quick jerk of his head in the direction of the Mexican.

"Say, that's quite an animal you've got out there. I'd be interested in buying your big yellow horse, he's a real beaut. How much would you take for him today," the gringo man said to the Mexican. The Mexican did not look at the gringo.

"He's no for sale," he said.

"I see, well I've got a little money and you know what they say, anything's for sale. Right, Amigo?"

"Habla Ingles? He's no for sale."

The Mexican continued not to look at the gringo and took a long gulp of his beer. The gringo flustered in the stare of the bartender.

"I see," he said and turned and shuffled back to his table in the corner, looking over his shoulder like a scolded dog as he went.

The Mexican watched in the mirror as the woman's excitement grew with the gringo man's approach, and then slowly waned as he sat and whispered to her; both stealing glances at the Mexican's back, seemingly unaware of the huge mirror that broadcast backwards all the go-ings on in the bar. The Mexican watched as she sized him up and down and repositioned herself in her chair in a way that caused his own back to straighten slightly and a tingling to dance across his shoulders. The gringo man began to petrify. He stiffened in his chair and fid-geted about the table, sipping his beer and setting it down and sipping it again. He could feel his new bride's demeanor shift from demure and the air instantly be-come positively charged with a surge of static electricity that forced erect the tiny hairs on his arms and the back of his neck. Everything about her suddenly crackled with a sexual current that she seemed to flick on as effortless-ly as flipping a switch on a wall. She had used this same flicking technique on him, in the beginning of their courtship, in an effort to throw him off balance. He would feel the tingling in the pit of his stomach and the slump fall across the base of his shoulders, his knees would jellify, and he would be rendered completely defenseless against any extravagances she might request of him. He knew how it worked and could often see it coming, but it was a perfected tactical maneuver that seemed to him completely invulnerable to any counter. She stood and smoothed her dress, arched the small of her back, and began her descent upon the unsuspecting Mexican. She moved along the wall, gazing curiously at the yellowed tapestry of clippings and photographs. Photographs of Mexicans riding donkeys, men standing proudly over dead deer, antelope and coyote; a tattered portrait of Pancho Villa himself. In a small wooden frame, partially obscured by a headline clipping proclaiming oil to have been found in abundance in the Permian Basin, she noticed a photograph of John Wayne posed in front of the Regar Agujero with a small man, who was not, yet looked oddly similar to, the bartender. She bent over and brushed away the newspaper, pushing her hips as far out into the room behind her as she could. Glancing around the room she giggled to herself, and said to no one in particular, "I'll be, that's John Wayne. I just love John Wayne." Every languid eye in the little bar had now fixated on every part of her. Beer soaked mouths hung agape. The air thickened and movement became more sluggish. The bartender moved with the movements of an ant swimming in thick warm sorghum, delirious and complacent in his euphoria. The Mexican stayed very still. He did not dare turn his head. She appeared at the bar, soft and quiet as an apparition, and oozed onto a stool and draped herself across the weathered walnut slab. The gringo man now slouched in his chair and crossed his legs at the knee and stared moodily at his shoe.

"Could I trouble you for two more of your coldest beers? Thank you shuga. It's so hot down here in this part of Texas," she said. The bartender stood paralyzed by the husk in her throaty voice.

"Darlin', the beers? Would you mind?"

The click of her red nails on the bar snapped him back and he turned and dug deep into the cooler, way in the back where he kept the coldest beers. Beer reserved for the day John Wayne or the like might wander into his fine establishment. She turned now and faced the Mexican as if she had just noticed him sitting there. The slit in her skirt exposing a bare thigh.

"How are you? You know what? I was white trash 'til I married Merle. It's true. Poor as a church mouse. Now I can have near anything I want. Merle Burwell Haywood the third. You ever heard of him? Can you believe they'd name three of 'em that?" The gringo woman laughed and reached over and patted the Mexican's leg, causing him to flinch.

"I just think it's dreadful, but oh well. Oil you know. West Texas oil wells. They got hundreds, maybe even thousands of 'em. Scattered all over like grasshoppers. Fat little grasshoppers all day long just sucking oil out of them dried up dusty ol' plains. Can you believe that? And now I'm a Haywood, don't that just beat all. From white trash to Haywood just like that. People say I look like Rita Hayworth. Do you think I do? I think it's funny my name's Haywood now, almost like Hayworth. Don't ya think? Why don't you come over and sit a while. Tell us some Spanish? Merle'll buy you a beer. "

The Mexican sat mesmerized by the flippant speech.

Frozen, staring at the gringo woman and straining to keep his eyes from darting back and forth between her gummy red lips and her bosom, bubbling up from her dress and spilling over in two salacious, creamy white mounds pressed together by her swanky posture atop the bar stool.

"Come on over. We're friendly." She touched the Mexican on the shoulder and winked as she stood and gathered her beers and made her way back across the room to the corner table and her miniature gringo man.

"Amigo, Pancho Villa says you are heading down a path with many twists and turns, and full of ruts from all the other wagons driving up and down it," the bartender said.

"Why don't you tell Pancho Villa to mind his own damn business? And dig deeper into that cooler this time and give me uno mas muy frio cerveza. The really cold ones," the Mexican said as he stood swaying in front of the bar.

He dug into his pocket and dropped his money down in front of his empty bottle of beer. The Mexican took his new frosty cold beer and shuffled with a slight limp across the room to the gringo's table.

"Howdy do. Merle Burwell Haywood the third, at your service," the gringo man said, offering out a hand, soft and bunched together in a tiny paw.

The Mexican squeezed the gringo's paw, mashing the pudgy little knuckles and grinding them together. "Say, that's quite a grip you got there amigo," the gringo said, pulling back his tiny mitt and massaging his fingers.

"I was a jockey, but no more. Took a fall at Agua Caliente. Broke my heep. I was runneen on the inside in second too. But, word gets around. Hard to fine a mount after sontheen like that."

"Oh, well yes, I do suppose so. Please, won't you join us," the gringo man said as he pushed a chair out with his foot.

The Mexican sat with a heavy thud. The beer and the heat now causing the Earth to rotate a bit faster, a mysteriously stronger gravitational pull tugging on his small body.

"I sure do admire your horse out there," said the gringo man. "He's quite a fine looking animal. How were you to come by him, was he a race horse?"

The Mexican took a sip of his beer and seemed puzzled by the gringo's questions, staring at him for an awkward time before answering.

"Which one?" said the Mexican.

"Pardon? Which one what? I only saw one horse outside tied to a post."

"Which one do you want to know? How did I come by heem or was he a race horse."

The gringo woman laughed and leaned in to the table dropping her chest low enough to cause immediate distraction.

"Oh, I think he's just gorgeous! Looks just like Trigger, you do know Trigger right, Roy Rogers's horse?" said the gringo woman.

"I heard of heem one time. He's that movie cowboy, no?" said the Mexican.

He had seen a television on several occasions but it never interested him enough to sit and look at one for any length of time. He felt too removed from the tiny images flashing colorless and distorted behind the bulbous glass.

"We'll, we've just married," interrupted the gringo

man, "eloped, as they say, to Las Vegas, Nevada." A proud toothy smile projected at the Mexican.

"I have never been there," said the Mexican.

He sipped awkwardly at his beer, his eyes wide and fixed on the wet ring left on the table by his condensing beer bottle and straining hard to keep himself from staring at the woman.

"Well, about that fine yellow pony outside, how did you say you were to come by him? He sure is a beaut," said the gringo man.

The Mexican's tongue loosened.

"He is a Palomino. There was a man over in Balmorhea. He had a big place. El rancho grande with many cattles and horses. He had a dream of racing his horses. They were pretty good, but no good enough to win. I told heem I would work his horses. I told heem about Agua Caliente. Runneen' in second against the rail. He give me a job, just like that. A bed in the bunkhouse. Three meals a day. It was nice. But, he got a daughter who was pretty. She was very pretty on the outside, on the inside, no so much. She was going to marry another man's son from one of the other gran ranchos. But I guess, she no love heem so much. She always say he was no a real man and she like a man who can handle a horse. She look at me and say, 'If a man can handle a horse like that what could he do to a woman?' Ay, yiyi. Anytime I see her come out of the house, I run and hide. I even bury myself one time in the hay up in the barn. I want notheen to do with her. Nada. She was uh, demasiado bonito para la virtud. When I say no to her, she go and tell heem that I say things to her that uh, well uh that I say things uh, los hombres sólo deben decir a las putas," he glanced nervously at the woman to see if she understood. She did not react and sat looking at her nails, her legs crossed at the knee and swinging her strapped high-heeled foot the way contentious women will do when they have become bored.

"The old man know I would no do sontheen like this. Sontheen to disrepect heem like this. But el rancho señora, his wife, she refuse to have me on the place. She tell heem I make her scared. That I was pervertido and I must vamanos. So, he give me 50 dollars, the saddle, and the Palomino and said gracias and adios."

"Well now, that's quite the tale," said the gringo man.

"Just the truth," said the Mexican.

"Do you always tell the truth?"

"I always try real hard, but no," the Mexican said as he reached and took his beer and gulped at the neck and drained the bottle and sat it out on the table in front of him and wiped his mouth across his shirt sleeve and smiled politely, a tiny spark of confidence igniting deep within him as he stared at the gringo woman.

"Well, I'd say that's put quite an end to that. You need another beer I see. What say we get three more bottles over here and have us a friendly little game of cards. You play cards friend?" asked the gringo man.

"I can play a leetle sontine," said the Mexican. The gringo woman suddenly engaged again.

"Oh, that sounds fun, I'll go get the beers." She stood and went to the bar and returned quickly and without fanfare with three more frosted bottles of beer.

"Well, as I say, we have just been in Vegas, and so I must fair warn, I'm getting awfully good at the five card draw," said the gringo man.

"I no too bad myself, sontine," said the Mexican.

"Oh, I love to play cards. Deal me in, Merle. This is

just so much fun. Isn't this just a hoot? I feel like I'm in a whole other country. And just think, it's still just Texas," the gringo woman said and giggled at herself.

The gringo man fumbled with a fresh new deck and dropped five crisp cards face down in front of each of them and sat the deck in the middle of the table and tapped it with his middle finger. The gringo woman quickly swiped up her cards and began mouthing softly to herself as she concentrated on them. The Mexican pushed the big Silverbelly back on his head and studied the gringo man carefully as he reached and surveyed the cards laid out in front of him. He laid the cards back face down on the table and took his new beer and took a long hard gulp from the neck, tilting his head back slightly and closing his eyes. He could feel the icy cold beer flowing the length of his throat and splashing into the pit of his stomach where it pooled momentarily, then flowed, sudden and rushing like a river fed by a mountain spring, down his arms to his fingertips and through his legs to where it crashed at the tips of his toes. He opened his eyes and dug through his pocket and removed all the money that he had pushed there earlier in the day. Sifting through the change he plucked a shiny silver quarter and dropped it into the middle of the table.

"Oh, well of course. The wager," the gringo man said and produced two quarters from his own pocket and dropped them out in the center of the table. "One's for you my dear. You're all ante'd up and ready to bet."

"Thank you shuga," the gringo woman said without taking her eyes off of her cards.

"I'm going to need two cards, myself," the gringo man said, discarding two cards from his hand and taking the deck and dealing himself two fresh ones.

"How about you, darlin'?" he said.

"Oh, I don't know. I guess, well, just give me four. Four new ones," the gringo woman said and dropped four of her cards into the center of the table.

The gringo man dealt her four new cards and looked at the Mexican. "And you?" he said.

"I no want no new ones. I like these ones," said the Mexican.

The gringo fanned out his cards and sat rubbing his chin as he surveyed his new hand.

"I do believe I'm going to raise a bit. I raise one more quarter."

"Ok," said the Mexican and he dropped another of his quarters down in the center of the table.

"Merle, I just don't know what I wanna do. But I think I'm doin' pretty good, put me in a quarter too," the gringo woman said and scrunched her nose and shoulders and grinned at the Mexican. "This is so much fun."

The gringo man dropped another quarter into the pile in the center of the table and said, "Well ok then, let's see what you got," and dropped his hand of a pair of fours down in front of him.

The gringo woman shrieked out, "Dadgummit, Merle," and dropped her hand of a pair of two's down on the table.

The Mexican looked at both of them for a moment and gently fanned down a hand of three queens; he raked the small pot to a pile in front of him, picked out a quarter and dropped it back in the center of the table.

"Looks like we have ourselves a game of high stakes poker here," the gringo man said and laughed at himself and shuffled his cards and flipped five more a piece around the table and sat the deck down and dropped two more quarters atop the Mexican's one.

"I think this time I take two new ones," said the Mexican and he took two hard gulps on his beer.

The sun began to sink in the western sky. Small rays dipped just below the roof of the porch and penetrated every blemish of chipped paint on the picture window in the front of the bar; a perforated glass curtain partially shielding those inside from the realities of their archaic world beyond. Tiny piercing rays pivoting on fulcrums of dust across the room, paraded on the tapestried walls like a kaleidoscope.

The Mexican had begun to metamorphose in his co-coon of beer. He was colorful and loose and laughing as though reunited with his long lost gringo friends. Re-united by some fate of happenstance in this, of all places, the Regar Agujero. The gringo woman made her way across the room and retrieved three more beers. The bartender no longer dug deep into the cooler. He had become acquainted with her beauty, lost himself in in-dulgent fantasies of her, and over time relapsed in the familiarity of her back to thoughts of his wife and the Asado de Bodas with rice and flour tortillas, and some horchatas that she would have for him when he arrived at home.

She did not notice the lukewarm beer and sat at the table sipping and looking at her cards.

"Well, amigo, it seems as though I'm all tapped out. Not a penny left in my pockets, it's all right there on the table," the gringo man said and laughed a loud exagger-ated laugh.

All three burst into a fit of laughter, the Mexican slapping his hand on the table and rocking back and forth in his chair. The lukewarm bottles of beer bobbled about and teetered on edge like seasick ship hands tossed about a deck on a rambunctious sea. The gringo composed himself and sipped his beer and stared at the Mexican through squinted eyes.

"This will have to be the last hand of the day. So, I'll tell you what, I do have one thing left and I'm ready to go all in or nothing. I'll bet that shiny new Buick out there against your yellow horse that I have the better hand. What say you to that?"

"Merle," the gringo woman said, "how on Earth are we gonna get home if you lose that car?"

"Now darlin' just don't you worry you're pretty little head about that. I'm sure there's a bus close by, and I'll just have daddy to wire me the fare. Besides, you only live once, right? It'll be a grand adventure."

A small fortune lay out in front of the Mexican in a pile that appeared to be far away. Far down the end of a hazy corridor flooded with soft golden light. He strained his eyes to focus on the cache of wealth, but the more he tried to focus the further away the fortune slid, deeper and deeper into the corridor. He walked toward it and reached out for it but it slid deeper still and he felt the heaviness in him pulling him back. Pulling him back into his chair with a force as though he would crash through the seat and through the floor and burrow into the desert caliche, deeper and deeper and further away from the wealth that he could not attain. The more he struggled to free himself from the grasp, the deeper he sank. Deeper into himself until at last he relented and slumped hard into his chair and fanned his cards and watched the faces of royalty dance in his hand. Two kings, a queen, a jack and a ten. He heard distant ancestral echoes deep in the recesses of his mind. Proud ancient Spaniards, matadors who had stood before El Toro waving madly at their destinies, thrusting steel fate at every charge. He saw Villastas charging savagely into Lajitas, hailing revolution at all cost, and he saw himself behind the wheel of the big Buick, the gringo woman nestled tight at his side, drunk in the fragrances of jasmine and lavender that caressed his face with the blowing of her auburn hair as he steered the big cruiser northbound. And just as they crossed the Nevada state line he heard somewhere faint and sure in the distance, the chanting buzz of the heads of flies on a thousand fools, "Royal flush, royal flush, royal flush."

"Ok," he said to the gringo man, "I bet," and he laid his cards out on the table in front of him.

The gringo man seemed to sober instantly and he straightened in his chair. He fanned his cards and looked at his wife and then the Mexican and then back at his wife. He grinned and laid his cards in the center of the table. Three aces and two kings; a beautiful spade, full boat flush.

"Well, it seems I have the better hand, amigo. And you darlin' have a pretty new yellow pony to look after."

The gringo woman squealed with delight and grabbed the little gringo man and kissed him about the face and ear and head as the Mexican strained to focus on the hand that lay before him on the table. He sifted his cards in search of his ace, but none was to be found. He reached for his beer as the gringo man and woman stood and gathered their belongings.

"It was surely a pleasure meeting you, friend. I assure you your horse will have a fine new home," said the gringo man.

The Mexican continued to stare at the cards on the table.

"Oh, Merle, I cain't believe I'm gonna be a cowgirl. How're we gonna get him home?" the gringo woman said.

"Well, we'll just lead him on up to Van Horn and stop and buy us a nice little ol' horse trailer. How's that sound, shuga? Easy as pie, darlin'. Easy as pie."

The Mexican sat petrified as the gringos shuffled to the door. The bright light exploding into the room momentarily and then they were gone. The barroom expunged of their presence like a startled awakening obliterates a nightmare. Leaving behind only a vague reminiscence of some grotesque misfortune, survived only to be contemplated as to whether it was a reality of past, present, or future consequence.

The Mexican gathered himself and stood and walked to the bar. He had kept a reserve in an inner pocket of his pants for just such occasion. It was not the first time he had played cards, and not the first time he had lost. He knew that cards was a game that demanded one have a reserve tucked away for the woes that from time to time must be diluted in the wake of misjudgment. He took some change from his pocket and dropped it on the bar in front of him.

"Uno mas cerveza. Uno mas muy frio cerveza," he said to the bartender.

The bartender shook his head and dug deep into the back of the cooler, as far into the back as he could reach. He pried the top off the frosty bottle and handed it to the Mexican.

"Gracias," said the Mexican as he took his beer and walked out of the barroom, the bartender following close behind.

The bartender and the Mexican stood on the front porch of the Regar Agujero. The Mexican sipped his ice-cold beer as they watched the big robin's-egg blue Buick disappearing like a mirage. The big Palomino on a lead rope tied to the bumper; a distorted mystical Rocinante loping along behind in the vaporous heat waves, dancing in the caliche dust of the road that led to the highway.

"Siento lo de tu caballo," said the bartender.

"Da nada. He was just a horse. It is the horseman that is the real prize. They bought me cerveza and I got to look at her all day. Almost like I spent the day with Rita Hayworth herself. Imagino que. That, mi amigo, will last forever. And besides, if they would have known anytheen about horses, they would have seen that the Palomino, he was almost twenty-nine years old. I'll eat my hat if he even makes it to Van Horn to get in a trailer."

The Mexican stepped off the porch into the hot evening sun and walked up the street. The proud black saddle slung over his shoulder; loud silver conchos on each side of the saddlehorn flicking a glint of white-hot light, popping and ricocheting off every surface he passed.

RIO GRANDE

I WATCHED the sun set on the Rio Grande today. The desert shined like gold. I looked over into Juarez at the shacks made of cardboard, tin, and treadless spare tires. I saw women – young and old and hard to discern – washing clothes in the red muddy water that slinked along the border, like some primordial serpent as it lapped at their legs and dampened the hems of their dresses. The outlines of their worn bodies silhouetted in the sunlight through the cheap fabric, semi-transparent and flimsy. I watched men stand and gaze across the border into what must have seemed to them like the Elysian Fields and I saw the deep lines in their faces that painted them with years far beyond those they had lived. And I watched young children dance in the water and splash all about their mother's laundry and squeal with laughter, unaware of the world that buzzed around them.

REDBIRD

I ONCE shot a rabbit with a Marlin 39A out in the Chihuahuan Desert amidst some mesquite brush. A big jackrabbit with black tips on his huge pointy ears and legs almost as long and skinny as mine. He was a flash of running wildfire until I whistled real loud and he froze like he'd hit a brick wall. Jackrabbits are funny like that, if you whistle loud enough sometimes they'll just freeze. Lay those big ears back on their shoulders and hunker down thinking they can't be seen. Right out in the open. They'll just sit there. My first shot hit him in the shoulder. Flipped him like a struck bowling pin. He tried to get up and run but he couldn't. Kept trying and trying to get up wondering why in the world his legs wouldn't do what his tiny brain was asking them to do. All instinct. Brain no bigger than a Burkett pecan. Even hit in the shoulder with his back broke, he still kept trying to up and run. My uncle said I should go over and crush his head with the heel of my boot, put him out of his misery. Misery I caused. I couldn't do it. So my uncle did. "Can't let him suffer," he'd said. We drove off and left that big old jackrabbit laying there with his skull mashed into the desert sand. "The coyotes'll gobble him up right quick," was the only eulogy offered that day.

When I needed to think I'd go melt crayons in a big mulberry tree on Ash Street. I'd climb the tree with a box of matches and a pack of Crayolas and spend hours letting the wax drip down the bark. Watching that beautiful technicolor cascade grow and become part of the tree, I felt artistic, expressive, and even a bit rebellious because I was playing with fire. I had gotten a BB gun, reluctantly given to me by my mother. A Daisy nonetheless. Lever actioned with a real wooden stock and grip. To this day I've never seen another like it. I don't know where my mother got it or who helped her pick it out, but it was a real beauty, quite the envy of Ash Street. I took to carrying it to the mulberry tree. One day I climbed up and sat perched in the fork of the trunk with my box of sulfur-tipped matches, my Crayolas, and the Daisy lever action, feeling like a miniature king. Armed and perched atop my mulberry throne I couldn't have asked for much more, when a flicker of red splashed my peripheral vision. A glorious redbird had landed on an adjacent branch and there he sat just watching me. His noble little head twitching back and forth in wonderment between the wax falls running down the bark and me, this strange creature entwined clumsily out of place in the branches of his big mulberry tree. I racked the lever of the Daisy and the redbird just looked at me. Looked at me then the wax and back at me again. He had plenty of time to fly away but he didn't, he just sat there watching. I was off balance and afraid I might fall out of the tree but I squeezed the trigger anyway. Just as soon as I did, I felt a jolt in the pit of my stomach. A dull kneading deep down in my gut and immediately I wanted to take it back. I wanted to reach out and flick that BB onto a new trajectory and send it ricocheting off through the branches like a tiny pinball. But it was too late. The little bird was gone. Vanished from the branch. One BB, aimed half-assed, dropped him off that limb with no fanfare at all. He just fell back and hit the ground simple as a matter of fact. I looked down through the branches and saw him lying there, dead as yesterday. I was shocked I'd actually hit him. I climbed down and scooped him up out of the dirt and brushed away the debris from his feathers. His bright scarlet body filled my hand like a gash. His once proud head now lay back limp against my thumb. I couldn't believe how pretty he was up close. The bold red feathers contrasting with the colors of a vivid butternut-squash yellow beak and the deep ebony accents on his crown and the tips of his wings. With his eyes closed lying back peaceful in my hand, he looked perfect. Perfect save for the tiny puckered BB hole right square in the middle of his chest. I carried him home in my pocket and buried him in a shallow hole in the flowerbed beneath a rose bush next to the porch. Marked it with a cross fashioned out of a broken popsicle stick bound with a rubber band. Never cared much for hunting after all that. Always seemed to me like killing just to kill.

DIRTY GREYHOUND

ASPHALT HIGHWAY stretching out into the night until it disappeared past the piss-yellow glow of the headlights. Big dirty Greyhound humming along, hovering above the white line like a hyped up junkie. We had gotten on in Oklahoma City. My mom, my brother, and me headed to New Mexico. The eight-hour drive would take fourteen as the bus would stop at every wide spot in the road that had a depot, or even just a convenience store with a sign – a picture of a bus on it that looked like a toy – screwed to a light pole. Towns with names like Elk City and Hereford. Eunice and Hope. Some places didn't even look like towns. Looked more like junk just scattered all about both sides of the highway. Abandoned buildings and rotted out trailer houses with tires or cinder blocks, or both, laying up on the roofs to hold down the tin when the wind blew especially hard. The wind could blow hard across a flat, stirring the ground upward; the sky like a sieve sifting dust back down to coat everything below in a fine chalky powder. Hard to imagine any life in some of these places, but the driver would announce each location and he'd pull in and stop and somebody would always appear out of the night to step off of or on to the bus. Either way, coming home or leaving home, the people looked hollow and distant. Zombified in the night shadows. Plodding through the motions as if pulled by some force they had battled long ago, grown complacent with the wearisome struggle, and simply surrendered to. I wondered if we stood out among them or if we were them, kindred on our journeys.

There was a particularly long stretch of highway on the plains of west Texas where the earth seemed to drop off into the black pitch just beyond the headlights. It was there in this blackness that the Greyhound's lights struck the chrome bumper of an abandoned car sitting on the shoulder. The driver's side back tire shredded and hanging from the rim, black and frayed as hag's hair. He appeared like an apparition in the high beams about a mile and half further up the road. The driver pulled the bus to a stop on the shoulder and opened the door.

The man was tall and lanky and swayed back and forth, then all at once teetered forward and lunged up into the bus. He looked like a cowboy. Pointy cowboy boots and jeans that hung down too long past the heel. A wide leather belt looped through his jeans and was fastened by a round silver plated buckle, the size of a serving plate, a bucking bull in the center with a tiny gold cowboy on its back. The driver spoke in mumbled tones so that you couldn't make out what he was saying. The man nodded a time or two and turned up the aisle, made his way about halfway and took an empty seat next to a large black woman; a nappy afro hairstyle stuck up in fuzzy nubs all over her head, a bright yellow slicker pulled up around her shoulders. She was either asleep or pretending to be so she wouldn't have to engage in some trivial conversation with any of her surrounding passen-

gers. The big dirty Greyhound eased off the shoulder
and back onto the highway. The low moan of the diesel
wound through all gears and she was once again humming along, the whining of the wheels against the midnight asphalt singing me back to sleep, sweet as any lul-
laby. It was somewhere on the bleakest stretch of blacktop between Amarillo and Hobbs that the ruckus started.
At first, singing. "Big City turn me loose and set me
free." Then "Working Man Blues." I opened my eyes just
as he started into "Tonight the Bottle Let Me Down".
The large black woman beside him pulled her jacket
completely over her head and did not stir again. The driver gave a stern warning for the man to hush it up. He
never took a hand off the big wheel and the Greyhound
didn't lose one mile an hour as he stared the drunk down
in his rearview. The cowboy quieted and slumped in his
seat with his knees high on the seat back in front of him.

The bus made about five more miles and the singing
started again. After a couple of bars the cowboy bolted
from his seat and whipped the belt from around his
waist. He pranced up and down the aisle like a vaudeville
character leading a parade, the belt with the giant buckle
whirling around his head, whipping like a chopper blade,
the lyrics of the great Merle Haggard bellowing out into
the night. We hunkered down as low as we could, trying
to disappear into the blackness of the floorboards. I felt
the bus ease to a stop and I stuck my head out just
enough to see the bus driver marching straight up the
aisle. When he reached the cowboy he yanked the belt
from his hand and spun him around, grabbing him by
the nape of his neck with one hand and a belt loop on
his jeans with the other. The cowboy hung in the grip of
the bus driver as the driver pushed him toward the front

of the Greyhound. An absurd western marionette flopping back up the aisle toward the door. The driver opened the door and gave the cowboy a good hard push down the steps. His boots stuck to the shoulder with an extra dose of gravity that drunks somehow seem to muster from the Earth's core. He stood leaning forward at an unnatural angle, yet managing to not fall face first into the asphalt as the door shut swiftly behind him.

The driver straightened his waist jacket and adjusted his hat and made his way back to where we sat and spoke to my mom, "Ma'am, there's an empty row up front, why don't you gather your things and ya'll come up and sit behind me?" Mom gathered up our things and we moved up the aisle, the cowboy standing on the shoulder pounding and kicking the door. The driver slid back behind the wheel and eased the big dirty Greyhound off the shoulder and back onto the highway, the diesel moaning through the gears with the groans of a tired, argumentative old man.

I sat up in the front seat right behind the driver that night and watched the cowboy in the side mirror burning down in the soft red taillights, black and crinkled like a spent wooden match, until the night swallowed him up and he was gone. And I wondered, for just a brief moment, where my dad was, who he was with, and what he had been doing while his sons and their mom dodged the whirling belt buckle of a drunk cowboy on a midnight dirty Greyhound running through the blackest and most barren part of west Texas. Then I laid my cheek against the cold of the window and closed my eyes and I didn't wonder any more.

HIGHWAY 90 WEST

TWO LANES Narrow shoulder too shallow really for a car. I pulled over all the way into the yellow grass that scorched on the exhaust and smelled sweet, like some distant smoldering piñon fire drifting on the crisp fall air. Two lazy black tarantulas crossed the highway. One headed north the other headed south. Rain. Coming or going. It always sets them on the move. In the background the Chisos Mountains severed the horizon with a jagged edge and soaked up the last blood orange sun of another twenty-four hours of my existence. Marathon, TX in the rear view mirror, Springsteen's "Ghost of Tom Joad," and home some five hundred-odd miles away.

STAGECOACH 105

WHEN I STEPPED into the room he was just sitting there with his back to the door. Nothing on but his boxers, staring at his feet. You can feel death in a room. You can feel it the same as a presence hidden in the dark. Watching you. You can't see it, but I swear you can feel it there. It lingers. Lingers all around a body until the body's in the ground.

The Stagecoach Inn sits on the south side of town in a row of cheap drive up to your door motels with names like Deluxe Inn and Motorlodge. When I was a kid you could pay fifty cents and swim in the Deluxe Inn pool all day, or at least as long as you could tolerate the random undercurrents of warm urine all the poor Chicano kids with fifty cents from redeemed pop cans and nowhere else to swim would contribute to the hyper-chlorinated water. When it's a hundred and fifteen degrees in a western sun and a hundred and five in the shade you could stay in the Deluxe Inn pool all day, warm undercurrents or not. The Stagecoach Inn was the nicer of these motels. The playground in the front made it look like a respectable place. A place to stay with your family, maybe your kids, until you got close to the swing set. The seats in the swings were cracked and dry rotted. Sun-faded resin broncos hung on stretched and rusted springs and would bump the ground if a kid weighed more than about sixty pounds, or just got caught up in the spirit of the wild west and got to bucking them too hard. It used to be a nice place with a really nice pool. A slide, diving board, everything. The kind of place where poor kids and Chicano babies couldn't swim all day pissing in the water for fifty cents. We didn't swim at the Stagecoach Inn. We swam at the Deluxe. All day. Fifty cents.

It was about five-thirty in the morning when the manager of the Stagecoach called and said he hadn't seen the guy in room 105 for three days. He'd knocked on the door; no one responded. He thought something might be wrong but he was afraid to go in and check. I hadn't even finished my first cup of coffee, and though it was stale and not hot enough to melt the powdered creamer that broke loose in clumps and splashed into the Styrofoam cup, it was still coffee. Any coffee at five-thirty a.m. is good enough for me, even bad police department coffee. I hated to pour it out just to drive out to the Stagecoach and see why some traveling salesman from El Paso, or some midlife crisis wanderer headed for Joshua Tree to try and reclaim the spirit of his wasted youth, wasn't answering his door.

I took the long way around Boyd Drive past the gravel pits where the ancient rock crushers stood and sputtered and coughed like gatherings of old men. Towering old men nearing their days of antiquation, huddled together gnashing and spitting out gravel like tiny bits of broken teeth piling around their feet, puffing great billows of smoke into the pink desert sky. I passed the big hot mix plant as it churned out miles of asphalt that would eventually cut through the parched caliche land-scape and carry thousands of travelers through and far away. I passed the spot where a man once flicked cig-arette ashes on me as I wrote him three citations, having initially intended a written warning until the ash stunt. I remembered arresting a man along the same stretch of road on a meth charge who was so large we had to use two sets of cuffs to get his giant doughy hands hooked behind his back. He was a nice guy and waited patiently as I fumbled with the assemblage of the adapted shack-les. I drove up Fiesta Street behind the Fiesta Drive-In with its broken marquee, advertising nothingness to a trailer park across the street inhabited by children who roamed shoeless and rode bicycles not intended for their gender and dogs with strong characteristics of the coyote and open windows with the violent crashings and shout-ings of deranged lovers. None of whom went to the drive-in movies.

I sipped my coffee and shifted in my seat behind the metal strike plate in my vest that covered my heart and caused a cool sweat to form in the middle of my chest even as frost caked the side mirrors of patrol unit eight five and I wondered if I could do this for nineteen more years.

The manager of the Stagecoach Inn was a nervous small-framed Hindu man who bore down on his back teeth, causing the tendons to stick out in his neck. His head looked like it was held onto his body with a web-bing of taut-stretched rubber bands. No telling how long he'd been waiting, pacing back and forth in front of room 105 cussing the police for taking so long; conjuring up all sorts of mayhem and conspiracy behind the door of the room while I drove around sipping bad coffee and contemplating my existence. He noticed me pull in and waved me over to the parking spot closest to the door. Two other more experienced officers had already gotten there and were waiting on me to arrive. They thought it would be funny to wait and make me go into the room first and possibly throw up on the floor. Give them something to talk about back at the twenty-year-old coffee pot that spewed out the stale coffee. The manager unlocked the door. I didn't throw up. Neither death nor the smell of it bothered me that much. I went without hesitation into the room, saw a figure in the dark sitting on the bed and said, "Sir? Hey, you on the bed. Let me see your hands." It was obvious that he was dead, but given the situation I couldn't think of anything more appropriate to say. "You ok?" Sounded a bit stupid. He wasn't ok. "Is anybody else in here?" sounded off as well. If anybody else were in that room with a ripe three-day-old corpse they more than likely wouldn't have just stepped out and said, "Oh, yea, I'm in here. Is there a problem, Officer?"

He was just sitting there with his back to the door. Nothing on but his boxers. Staring at his feet. Eyes wide open. Just staring at his swollen purple feet. Swollen like two giant gorged grapes stuck onto the ends of his legs. He was a Mexican from Texas, married and about sixty-five years old. A wedding ring had sunken into his swollen finger almost disappearing into the gorged flesh. His hands had hung down so long they had filled with his stagnant blood, giving them an inflated, puffy cartoonish look. The hands of a caricature. The wedding ring would have to be cut off with wire cutters later in the morgue. I don't know why but I remember thinking, 'til death do us part. It's funny what can roll through your mind in awkward moments. How random, nonsensical thoughts can invade your rational thinking and cause you to see into some strange other dimension where death manifests itself as a giant pair of wire cutters and clips the strand that binds your soul to your mate's. Where had she been and what had she been doing as this man, her loved one, her soul mate, sat alone on the edge of a bed in a cheap motel staring at his unkempt giant purple feet, feeling his life seep from his worn out body?

A quick look around the room squelched all crime scene drama. Nothing out of place. No signs of forced entry or foul play. All his money was still in his wallet. The TV on, strobing blue tinted soft porn along the walls and the ceiling. The thermostat set on eighty, an invisible pumping steam locomotive circulating hot rancid air. On the nightstand next to the bed lay twenty Marlboro Red cigarettes positioned in a perfect line beneath the soft golden glow of the lamp. An easy reach from a lying position in the bed; twenty ten-penny coffin nails all in a neat row just waiting for the carpenter of death to tack down the lid on this guy's coffin. A wastebasket sat on the floor next to the bed and bubbled over with empty cans of Mello Yello soda. Bright neon green aluminum spilling out in high contrast against the brown shaggy carpet. There must have been a whole case of those sodas with only a few left unopened. A defiant dare. A ritualistic manifestation of a lack of self-control. When the coroner finally arrived she slung out her giant plastic bag with the same technique as a maid flinging out a sheet over the bed. The black plastic waving out briefly like a flag and then floating softly down beside the body. She asked me to put on a pair of disposable plastic gloves and help her push the man back flat so she could zip him up and haul him off. A tidy zip-locked package, delivered to a cold slab to be callously dissected, cause determined to satisfy the state's requirements for an "unattended death procedure," and stapled back together in grotesque distortions for presentation to whoever might appear to claim what was left to be claimed. Rigor mortis had set in and when we rocked him back onto the bed he stayed in a seated posture. He looked like a giant bug drawn up from the shock of its own instant death. Knees drawn up, feet sticking up, and eyes wide open fixed on the ceiling. His face in a frozen surprise. His knees creaked when straightened as if hung on rusty hinges and his arms levitated inches above his sides. As his body straightened some air that had been trapped in his lungs by his seated position rattled out of him. The escaping of one last trapped and frightened ghost clamoring for freedom from its unlocked cage before the door slammed shut for all eternity. I've heard that raspy last breath called the death rattle, and even if you've heard it before it'll make you damn near jump right out of your skin every time. As I watched his face disappear behind the zipper of his plastic cocoon it occurred to me that at some time in the near future someone would be sleeping in this room. Sleeping, or God knows what else, on this bed. Taking shelter in this dank sepulcher of brown shag and blue strobing soft porn that had so unceremoniously drawn the life out of this man. I couldn't help but feel sorry for him. No glorious legacy here. No valiant hero's battle cry meeting death head on in a furious charge of honor. No peaceful slipping into the ages surrounded by adoring loved ones. Alone. Nothing. Just Marlboros, Mello Yello, and porn.

Myocardial infarction. Death by lack of self-control. Case closed.

I stood in the doorway of room 105 at the Stage-coach Inn and watched the coroner's van drive away, past the swimming pool and the little swing set and the faded resin broncos. The smell of the lifeless Mexican traveler lingered and I could taste the faint taste of death on my tongue mixed with stale coffee and powdered creamer from the precinct coffee pot and I knew I could not do this for nineteen more years.

LA CAVERNA

SOMEBODY KILLED a vagrant woman - a prostitute it was said - and stuffed her up in the box spring beneath a bed in the La Caverna Motel. Laced her right up through the wood where you couldn't see a thing when you looked under the bed. People checked in and out of that room for a week. Coming and going. Sleeping, and God knows what else, in that bed and all the while never the wiser. It finally started to stink so bad people complained. Asked to be switched to a new room.

"What kinda place is this," they'd say.

"We shoulda gone to the Super 8. Chains you know. More dependable. Consistent or there wouldn't be so damn many of 'em still in business."

"Local culture my ass," they'd say. "Same architect who built the hotel James Dean stayed in out in Marfa when he filmed GIANT. Who gives a rat's ass. GIANT was filmed half a century ago and this dump was probably here half a century before that."

"The rooms stink to high heaven and the beds are a lumpy mess. Shoulda stayed at the Super 8."

Maids went in and scrubbed everything down supposedly, you know how that goes. Vacuumed the floors they said. Looked all around the room, in the closets for some trapped animal. Even got down on their tired old knees, all the way on the floor and looked under the bed. Nothing there. We don't have no idea. So, a cop came in and looked around for a minute. Flipped the bed over and what do you know, Jane Doe naked and rotten. They tore the La Caverna down. Hand made Mexican tile in the lobby. Hand scraped vigas in the ceilings. All of it. Tore it to the ground. Never found out who the woman was or who it was killed her. Always wondered if anybody ever even missed her.

THE SACK MAN

THE SACK MAN rode the fruit trains that rattled past the North Forty trailer park at night. Lurking in dark corners of ambling boxcars clacking through the lowlands of mesquite and purple sage that perfumed the air. He'd come down from the north through the Bible belt and across the plains of Oklahoma where he crossed into Texas. The rails were easy in west Texas. Often running long stretches across vast open seas of desert dotted with prickly pear and yucca and mesquite brush with long yellow beans dangling in the moonlight, flickering like decorations on scraggly Christmas trees. Lives that evolved there were hardscrabble. Happenstance creatures adept at impoverished living. Creatures of the night that hid from the scorch of the sun and slinked from their cover into the silvery glow of the moon, to stalk and feed upon each other like ghouls. This is where the Sack Man found kinship. Brother to the viper coiled in the creosote bush and the starving coyote with wild darting eyes and a hide stretched taut over a rib cage, punching through the fur like an internal prison, locking in an intrinsic savagery.

Coyotes were kindred. Dogs a different story altogether. The Sack Man steered clear of dogs. Dogs bark and carry on and alert anyone in earshot of goings on that aren't familiar. More times than he could remember even the smallest of dogs would key on his presence lurking outside a child's window and raise enough of a ruckus until lights in the house began to come on. Occupants stirred. Curtains pushed aside and faces pressed against windowpanes peering blindly into the night. It was just easier to steer clear of houses with dogs. On a good night if he hit a stretch with no dogs it was said that the Sack Man could stuff sixty, sometimes sixty-five kids. He was quick and right down to business. Slip through the window silent as a vapor, cut the hangy-downs off your ears with a pair of tin snips, and leave them on the dresser for your parents, then throw you in his giant burlap tote sack with all the other ear-lobeless children of the desert and sell you to the street vendors in Juarez, Mexico, never to be seen or heard from again.

But the Sack Man steered clear of dogs. You could be sure of that. If you had yourself a real good dog you could sleep sound. No worries. I never could keep a dog for long; the Sack Man maintained a high level of threat in my tiny world within the boundaries of the North Forty. My ear lobes buzzed in a constant state of tingle at the thought of his tin snips snipping them from my ears. See, I always liked the idea of a dog. The ever loyal companion standing fast by your side through the good and the bad, but for some reason all that stuff never seemed to stick with me. Hotdog was no exception. He was a black and tan Basset hound mix, long as a two by four and no taller than a coffee can. He lived mostly in a shallow dugout hole in the dirt beneath the front porch of the trailer. When he wasn't sleeping, he roamed.

There wasn't a fence in Eddy County that could hold him in or keep him out. Arching his back and nearly bending himself in two he would weasel under any enclosure. He'd squeeze right through with nothing but mischief on his mind and spend an evening raping and pillaging the North Forty. He'd skip around and screw one here and one over there, then rip the head off an unsuspecting chicken for dinner before trotting on back home, nose in the air, fully satisfied and ready for a good night's sleep under the front porch. It did not take long for the phone calls to begin. Neighbors had to be calmed. Chickens had to be replaced. Hotdog had become a menace. And once more, worthless as a frontline defense against the Sack Man. With Hotdog off of his post most every night, the trailer was wide-open, easy pickings. Might as well have just pushed up the windows, cut the hangy downs off your own ears, sacked yourself up, and waited.

With the Sack Man on the rampage and the trailer completely vulnerable there was no other option. Hotdog had to go. We needed to regroup and refortify. Secure the perimeter with a respectable dog. A dog of character and loyalty. Maybe even an AKC registered something or other worthy of a noble moniker like Buck or Duke. Not some hapless grifter mutt who could inspire no other name than that of a tripe-filled lunch meat, and on top of that thought only of himself and his insatiable appetites. It was decided. Hotdog was to be taken away. Uncle Joe was a man of clarity. A man of action and swift decisiveness and the owner of a metallic green Chevy Chevelle, into which Hotdog was loaded and driven twenty miles out on highway 62/180 to a dirt road behind the county landfill. Uncle Joe pulled the

Chevelle to a stop and let the engine run while he leaned across the seat and opened the door and let the dog out. A pat on the head and a hearty good luck and that was that. Problem solved. Three days later, Hotdog trotted back up the drive, curled up under the front porch and fell fast asleep, the conquests of his grand adventure rolling through his simpleton dog dreams. He was home, and, come to think of it, starving. More dead chickens. His next adventure found him thirty miles into the desert in the opposite direction of the landfill. Ought to be interesting. A little more challenging this time. Four days later with sore paws and drooping ears he flopped into the dugout beneath the porch and slept for twelve hours straight.

It was fast becoming apparent that the only thing that was to rid the number 25 space at the North Forty Trailer Park of Hotdog and his troublesome ways was a twelve gauge pump and a stout dose of double-aught buckshot to the back of his head. There wasn't any more time to waste. The Sack Man was still about and rumor had it that he was working southeast New Mexico. Our dog situation had to be resolved. The dog was loaded up one more time and driven back out the highway. Just outside of town a narrow stretch of pothole-afflicted blacktop led into a wide stretch of desert, dotted with gas wells standing like huge mechanical grasshoppers. Massive steel heads bobbing up and down pecking at the parched ground. Amidst the grasshoppers, caliche pits lined with broken beer bottles glistening in the sun like remnants of ancient stained glass windows pockmarked the scorched and dehydrated earth. This is where Hotdog was to meet his fate. His menacing carcass left to be picked clean by the buzzard. His bones bleached by the sun and scattered about by the coyote that would crack open the smaller ones and suck the marrow. The car came to a stop and the doors opened and the dog hopped out and surveyed the pit with a sniff. A shell slid smoothly into the firing chamber of the twelve gauge. Hotdog heard the sharp familiar click of the safety and at a casual lope bounced around to the back of the car out of sight. His big clumsy head to the ground, he watched underneath the car as the boots crunched across the gravel. As the footsteps closed in, the dog trotted around to the front of the car and sat back down. His head lowered and watching the boots as they stopped at the back of the car. Now Uncle Joe was a friendly enough character, but patience was not always said to be one of his greater virtues. He stood for a moment at the back of the car, shotgun in hand, and called and whistled for the dog, then crouched down and peered under the car. Hotdog lay at the front bumper staring back at him. Uncle Joe moved quickly down the side of the car. He rounded the front fender and lowered the shotgun. The dog was gone. He stooped again and looked under the car to see Hotdog at the back bumper. Uncle Joe darted toward the back of the car and Hotdog darted toward the front. Master and dog now running circles around the car, stopping momentarily to catch a breath and assess the other's position then taking up the chase again. First running clockwise then counter-clockwise. Then a fake counter-clockwise to clockwise. Then stopping. Then an all out sprint round and round the car, caliche dust hanging in the air like a soft mist, short fat Basset hound legs and long flopping ears flailing wildly in a dead out, run-for-your-life sprint. Cowboy boots slipping and sliding in the loose gravel, colorful curses in all degree spewing forth in a steady cadence. Hunter and hunted both panting with hanging tongues, finally coming to a stop. One at the front bumper one at the back. The dog breathed heavily, peeking his snout out from behind the front tire, assessing the danger. As the boots began to move again, Hotdog could go no more. He crouched onto his belly and scooted his long fat body up under the car and dropped with a thud in the dirt. Uncle Joe kicked gravel, threw gravel, opened and slammed the doors, started and revved the big V-8 until the rods wound tight enough to snap, then knelt and tried to sweetly coax the dog from under the car. He would not budge.

It had become apparent that there was going to be no clear shot at this particular dog. He was obviously not going to just stand still and get his head blown off, and shooting a twelve gauge shotgun blast up under the car was not an option. You might hit the gas tank and cause an explosion. You might hit the oil pan. Oil would leak out onto the desert floor and you'd be walking the ten miles back to town.

Uncle Joe leaned back against the car and propped the twelve gauge against the trunk, took a can of Skoal from his hip pocket and mashed a pinch of the peppery wintergreen snuff into the lining of his lower lip. The dog eased out and slinked around to the back of the car, rocked back on his haunches and sat staring up at him.

"We'll, I guess just get back in, you son of a bitch," Uncle Joe said. "A bonafide son of a bitch if I ever saw one."

The Chevelle eased out onto the blacktop and shrank to a speck before it disappeared over the horizon. Thirty minutes later Hotdog flopped down in the dugout beneath the front porch and slept without stirring until morning.

That summer it was said that the Sack Man had moved on. Rode the rails out to California and disappeared up into the Northern Pacific states. Some say he slipped beneath a freighter car and got cut clean in two and dragged up the line until there was nothing left of him. Others say he was burned alive in a trash fire in a landfill when his sack got hung on a rusty car door. Most people say he was just torn apart and devoured by a loyal pureblood German shepherd named King.

SUGARBOY

"BRING ME SOME SUGAR boy. This coffee's bitter as wormwood. I can hardly start without my coffee."

The old man sat in a plaid wingback chair, worn in the places where his arms rested and soiled where his oily hair pressed against the fabric as he sat for hours on end staring out the window. Grey eyes, distant and sunken in sallow cheeks. The skin of his face hung loose and droopy, clumsy like the jowls on an old, loyal hound. His hands lay neatly folded on his lap, the nails on each of his fingers yellowed and hardened to a thickness that rebuked clippers and grew longer than a man's nails should. Had his hands not been arthritic and gnarled, his fingers twisted as willow tree roots, they might have looked a bit feminine folded in his lap with the nails grown long. He'd been sitting since four-forty-five waiting for the sun to rouse the boy. It was unclear as to whether he had slept in his bed, awakened and dressed himself and shuffled down the hall and took up the chair, or whether he had slept right where he sat, shoes on and both feet stuck fast to the floor. It was getting so that the boy could no longer tell and had since stopped pondering the thought. It really made no difference to the boy as to where the old man slept, so long as he slept and left the boy to do the same.

The room in which the old man sat day after day after day was stale, monochrome and ashen and devoid of any manifestations of the old man's personality. On the front wall stood a television cabinet constructed of particleboard covered in laminated plastic that was printed with a grain pattern to simulate fine wood. The picture on the TV hissed a constant snowy flashing of archaic cowboys. Usually Festus and Marshall Dillon, or the Barkley's of *The Big Valley*. Sometimes *The Rifleman*. The Rifleman was his favorite. He would never say he liked television, but he would turn his head with slight interest when Lucas McCain flickered across the screen. He'd be quick to deny watching it if asked. He refused to be accused of interest in such menial habits.

The boy had come out of his room and was standing in the kitchen in nothing but his white jockey shorts, eating the icing out of Oreo cookies and throwing the wafers in the trash. He was ignoring the old man. He had heard the story more times than he cared to remember, and as the old man continued his descent into dementia the story had become an everyday occurrence. Some days multiple tellings would spill from the old man, each growing more dramatic than the one before; details distorting and crescendos bellowing and echoing through the halls of the little house.

It always started the same way. "Them sons of bitches just think I'm an old man. That's all they see. Just an old man with thin blood. Cold in the middle of June. This sweat stained yellow t-shirt under my shirt and a stale sweatshirt over that, and still chilled to the bone smack dab in the dead of summer. Who do they think they are to take my keys anyway? Trick a man out of his keys. Disrespectful little bastards. I still sit out in that

Pontiac. In the drive with the windows down. I listen to those swallows in the eaves. I can hear the aphid wings flutter through the leaves on the pecan tree. Feel the sap drizzling down like a mist on my arm. Take this Tommy gun .45 caliber and lay it up on the front seat and you get this load to Fort Sill. And don't you stop for nobody, you hear. Nobody, save for a colonel what orders you to. Anybody else tries and stop you, you shoot 'em with that Thompson sub machine. Now I'm counting on you, Sergeant. That's whose keys they stole. Tell me I can't drive, phshaw. They thought I didn't know what they's up to. Her cattin' around like she was. I'd catch him stealing looks at her right in the middle of the sermon at church. Don't that just beat all. The preacher standing up there preaching about keeping yourself right with the Lord and him over there lusting after my wife. I'll admit it did take me a while to catch on. But I just had a feeling something wasn't right. It was colder that night than I had planned on it being. I asked him if he'd mind riding me out there around Blevins Pond about ten miles out F.M. 285. Told him I'd been out there fishing for crappie, everybody fishes out there for crappie and them little white bass. Anyhow, I told him my battery went dead on my old truck and would he mind ridin' me out there and giving me a jump. Of course he said sure thing. We made a bunch of small talk drivin' out there, weather, local gossip, and what not. He didn't have no idea that I knew. It was kind of hard for me to just ride along and talk to him knowing I had my mind set on blowing his damn fool head off. I took that little .22 pistol out and sat it on my lap once we reached the pond and he could see that my truck wasn't out there. He saw that pistol and I know he damn near pissed hisself. Tried acting dumb to everything and I just shut him up right quick. Said I knew what was going on and there wasn't no sense in him playing me for stupid and trying to talk me out of doing what I come out there to do. He finally admitted to the whole thing. Told me how it started. Of course told me it just happened. They'd never planned to, it just did. He was at least decent enough to spare me any details, even though I told him I'd blow his left nut off if he didn't tell me some of what they'd done. He just said sorry, he wouldn't do that. I'd just have to shoot him. He wasn't going to talk bad about her. He told me she was lonely. He said that was really what got them to talking. She was just lonely was all and needed somebody who would listen to her. He said he felt the same way most of the time and that's how they started. Just talking. I couldn't figure out what the hell he was talking about. She needed somebody to talk to? That didn't make a lick of sense to me; she talked all the time. Never shut up as a matter of fact. Got to where I just had to tune her out sometimes to keep from going stark raving mad. I never could hear my own self think for her talking. Anyhow, I'd heard enough so I got him out and walked him over to the edge of that pond. He never begged me or anything. He did pray a little, softly under his breath. That made me real mad. I'm a God fearing man myself and me and God both knew he had it coming, and I didn't like him trying to get God sided up with him in this whole deal. I wasn't the one who'd done no wrong. I didn't ask for any of this. I walked him right up to the edge of that pond and took that pistol and stuck it right on the side of his head and pulled the hammer back. It clicked three times and he flinched hard at each little tick it made. I stood there for what seemed like an hour. My blood pumping so hard it was ringing in my ears. Made me dizzy. And then, all of the sudden I heard it, loud and clear as if someone had walked right up behind me and said it in my ear. The voice of God as sure as I'm sitting here. "Don't you shoot him. Do not do it." Just so clear it made me flinch. Well I knew I couldn't do it then. Knew I'd never be forgiven for it. So, I thought about it for a minute, and then I made him strip off all his clothes. Every damn stitch. His little old pecker so shriveled up in that cold it looked like a peanut. A little old wrinkly peanut trying to crawl back up inside his pale blue body to get away from all that cold. And it was cold. Damn cold lookin' back on it. I took his keys and his truck and all his clothes; socks, shoes and everything and told him I'd leave it parked over there on the square in front of the courthouse. Said all the kids like to go over there in the evenings and sit around and visit so there'd be a lot of folks out to keep an eye on it for him. Figured a ten mile walk of shame in this cold would help him to get his mind right and think twice next time about trying to offer comfort to lonely married women.

"When I got home she was sitting there on the divan. She looked up at me and said, 'Did you kill him?' I just saw red. I couldn't speak so I just hauled off and slapped her three good hard slaps right across her face. That third one cracked like a pistol shot. Made her nose bleed a little. When I saw the blood, I stopped. Her cheek flamed up bright red in an instant like it had burst out a fire. She just sat there and stared at me. A little tear welled up in her eye and spilled over and ran down her cheek. Looking back I think it was more sadness than pain from her cheek. Neither one of us ever mentioned anything else about it. Not one word in all those years.

That's the only time I ever laid a hand to a woman before or since. From the minute I did it I wished I could've taken it back."

It was not until her death that the old man had discovered the letters. One afternoon, given to a bout of melancholy and feeling that a bit of a change might lift his spirits, he decided to rearrange the furniture in his bedroom. He pulled the stack of yellowed envelopes, bound in a length of satin ribbon, from a hole in the wall hidden by a pried-out piece of paneling behind their dresser. He felt sick when he read them. Sick with a sadness that churned in his gut and kneaded his insides to a point where he almost gagged. As he read he could not force himself to deny that he had not loved her with a love that was proclaimed so eloquently in those letters. Unselfish. Unconditional. Kind and giving, never asking anything of her. Just simple proclamations of a love that she need always know was felt for her; to know that she was truly loved in the deepest purest way. The letters simply begged her to know that, nothing more. He could not help but envy the man that he had harbored such hatred for. The man who had loved his wife the way she had deserved to be loved, the way he never could seem to. As he read, a thought began to fester in his mind. Had she written him back? What had she said to him? Had she pledged her love for him the way these letters pledged his for her? Or had she simply hidden them away and not replied? He knew he would never know, both of them were gone now. He had figured all along that his wife loved him because she had stayed. He ached at the thought that she stayed because she was supposed to. Because that's what women of her generation did. They stayed. After he had read all the letters, he retied the bundle with the satin ribbon and placed it back in the hole in the wall and tacked the loose panel down with two small nails and slid the dresser back into its place and had not moved it again.

As the rant continued, and began to deteriorate, the boy crept silently down the hall and into the old man's room. The closet door squeaked at the hinge and he froze and listened for the old man to stop talking and call out for him but the old man never missed a beat and the boy stepped into the closet and climbed atop a small wooden footstool. He stretched onto his tiptoes and felt around the top shelf until his hand brushed the cloth. He pulled the heavy lump down and stepped from the closet and laid it out on the old man's bed. Wrapped in the cloth lay a .22 pistol. A nine-shot, H&R single action revolver with a grip that was slightly yellowed and marbled like bone. Its blued finish glistened and the boy caught a whiff of linseed oil. He breathed it in deeply and listened as the old man's thin voice echoed distantly through the little house.

"I've seen 'em go from horse and buggy to rocket ship on the moon. What now? What the hell are you supposed to do now until you die? Just sit and wait I suppose. I'd have me a short beer while I wait, if I had one. Or a Pepsi would do all right. God I do miss her so."

The boy now stood silent behind the chair, the barrel of the .22 inches from the base of the old man's skull.

"Boy? Are you there? Bring that sugar, boy. I can hardly start without my coffee."

THAWING OF A RELIABLE MAN

THE ADVERTISEMENT had hung in the window for three months. Every day since noticing the ad Ethom would take his lunch by the front window and study backwards the lithographed images. The sun glistening through the imperfect glass and thick yellow paper, illuminating the sketches mountain scenes, lakes, and winding rivers in crude reverse distortions. Promising acres of hardwoods the likes of birch, alder, and black walnut, and sweet peppery stands of black jack pine all for the taking. Ethom had often stopped on the outside of the window and studied the prints, envisioning himself standing high atop a peak or struggling to fell a massive birch. The bite of the ax sinking into the flesh of the tree trunk and pulling out thick chunks of succulent melon wood. He could smell black jack just looking at the poster and at times when he closed his eyes he imagined a breeze so sweet and crisp that it took his breath. He would catch himself with a slight gasp and scan the mercantile showroom in hopes that no one had witnessed his daydreaming. Daydreams of grandeur; youthful lust that impregnated the minds of men who had not quite fully matured into the realm of reliable.

It was at the close of business one evening that Mr. Tomes, without warning, removed the advertisement from the store window and dropped it into the waste-basket behind the counter, where it drifted slowly downward and landed perfectly unscathed atop the refuse. Ethom promptly removed the ad and asked Mr. Tomes if he could have it. With a look of slight confusion Mr. Tomes replied, "Of course. Just don't hang it back in here. I'm tired of looking at it." Ethom carefully folded the ad and tucked it into the inside pocket of his vest. At the close of business he moved swiftly about his tasks. Sweeping the floor, straightening the stock on the shelves, tallying the day's receipts, and recording their balances in the worn ledger that Mr. Tomes had insisted on not replacing for the last several years past its obvious state of disrepair. He locked up the store front, as he was the only employee that Mr. Tomes had entrusted with a key, and hurried up the street toward the flat and Ania, whom he knew would be waiting for him with a hot meal of potatoes, red cabbage, cornbread, and piping hot coffee. If he were lucky this evening, she had made beans. Beans with a thick cut of pork fat-back for the rich salty flavor and the grease that softened the beans to a tenderness that melted in the mouth and sufficiently filled the belly. The street was the usual fare. Buzzing with the ambitious. Replete with uniformity. A crawling mass, scratching and clawing for opulence. Ethom made his way through the throngs and bounded up the stairs to the flat and burst through the door with a fanfare that startled Ania.

"Ethom, what is it? Are you alright? What's happened?"

"Alright? I'm much better than alright. Come, sit, I want to show you something."

The ad was the first Ania had seen or heard of

Ethom's longing for a life outside the comforts of town. She could plainly see that the ad had ignited in him a desire for what he described as a life of promise. Independence. A life where he could be a man. His own man, not just a prosperous man's merchant boy. She listened over dinners and lunches and nights when their heads lay touching on the fat feather pillows, as he incessantly rambled about the beauty of the mountains and the streams that glistened like opalescent ribbons cutting through pastures lush as deep green velvet. The abundance of wildlife and game. Turkey, elk, venison, quail, all for the taking. She sat patiently as he paced back and forth in front of her chair, promoting the advertisement with the passion of a Pentecostal preacher.

Ethom Juhlin and his wife Ania had settled in Spokane, Washington, having left Sweden after numerous failed attempts at a meager farm. Ethom bartered his acreage for their passage across the Atlantic aboard the steamship *Campania*. With every intention of reaching and settling in Seattle, he had been left with just enough for himself and Ania to ride the Transcontinental to the Northern Pacific as far as Spokane. Their long and treacherous journey had concluded on the front steps of a boarding house six blocks from the Tomes Mercantile, in a two-room flat – with a shared bathroom at the end of the hall – overlooking the hustle and bustle of the city street below. Ethom had found work as a clerk in the mercantile and spent his days in the employ of Mr. Isaac Tomes, a fair yet stoic little man who clutched tightly every cent that graced his palm and had no intention of giving an upper hand, or an unnecessary opportunity for advancement, to any of his employees. Ania said it was a good beginning. Ethom said he feared it was the beginning of the end. Day after day Ania watched Ethom from the window as he would leave the flat and make his way to the mercantile. Once he was out of sight she would sip warm tea and nervously study the advertisement. Ania was a patient and generous wife. And though she loved their life in the city, she loved Ethom more. Loved him from first glance. Latched on like a piglet to a sow's teat and didn't seem to be going anywhere that he wasn't. Once the decision was made, she had to admit to a certain excitement in the adventure of it all.

The year passed quickly once the cabin was completed. Summer gave way to fall with the forest exploding in an array of color that was hard for Ania to articulate. The work had been diligent. Cords of split jack pine stacked neatly to cure and season in the sun just yards from the cabin door. Ania had insisted on tidiness and would not have stacks of firewood haphazardly piled up around her home. She handled the small hatchet well and had contributed an enviable pile of kindling to the collection of wood. Ania did not like to be cold and had informed Ethom that it was the kindling that kept the fire hottest and she felt she could never have too much at hand. Ethom would often find her at the wood pile, singing and chopping wrist-sized pine limbs into splintery, resin-filled kindling, then organizing the firewood by size into an intricate, accessible architecture of fuel. She required order, for in order there is efficiency, in efficiency there is peace of mind. Much game had been harvested. Venison, elk, turkey, cured in salt and hung in a smokehouse six feet square and five feet high with a solid door and a stiff latch to keep out the wolf, the coyote, and the occasional small black bear, whose hunger gave it the nerve to disregard the danger of human interaction. Ethom had proven himself quite the hunter, having traded a set of silver spoons, handed down by his grandmother, and two bottles of Brännvin Vodka for a Hawken 50 caliber rifle, a big buttermilk dun pack mare, and enough black powder to see him through winter.

The isolation felt by Ania while Ethom was away, deep in the wilds of the forest chasing the bugle of elk or at the rocky base of the mountain climbing in the tracks of the bighorn sheep, would always bring about melancholia. The nights alone in the cabin played tricks on her mind and made her sleep restless and her heart long for the flat and the shared bathroom down the hall. The howling of wolves deep in the night seemed to grow ever closer and as the moon's glow drifted among big smoky clouds, shadowy figures lurked at every window and rattled the door, testing the latch. The wind. Sharp drafts of cold had begun to pierce the earthen chinking in the walls of the little cabin. Many nights Ania lay feeling the sting on her face like needle pricks and she longed for Ethom's return when he would crawl beneath the heavy quilts and she would lie in his arms and feel the warmth of his bare skin against hers and cling to him until late in the muted warmth of morning. Then winter. An all out onslaught of frost and snow and bitter cold that ached deep in the bones. The mountain seemed to erupt in violent revolt against the intrusion of all living things, an assault of a magnitude that instantly depressed Ania and secretly caused Ethom concern though he would not show it.

"I do not know if I can withstand this. I cannot remember ever having been this cold. I miss the flat, Ethom. I miss town. There, I've said it," Ania said, amidst the frigid howling moan of the night.

"You mustn't think this way, Ania. This is our home now. We cannot simply go away when it becomes uncomfortable. We are prepared to winter. We have food and enough fuel to heat for longer than any winter can last. Come, stay by the fire. It will be warmer tomorrow and the day after and every day until it is summer. You'll see. Sit here, by the fire," Ethom said, trying to comfort her.

"I do not want to sit by the fire. I want to bury myself beneath the quilts and not awaken until summer. Maybe not at all."

"Ania, don't say such things."

"I am too cold to speak to you any longer."

Ania crossed the room and crawled into their bed beneath the mountain of quilts. She burrowed her head into the bedding where she could breathe but not be seen. Ethom sat up in the night dozing in a chair and tending the fire until dawn, feeding kindling until he had produced a small, near incinerating blaze. When Ania awoke he told her of his plan to make one more hunt before hanging his Hawken above the mantle until spring. She pleaded with him not to leave, but he reassured her that it would be a short hunt and that it would give them more than enough food to not have to conserve during the season's harshest weeks. Ania fell deeply sullen as she watched him disappear up the trail and into the trees.

On his sixth day in the wild, Ethom tracked a large cow elk deeper into the backside of Calispell Peak than he had intended to hunt. The sky darkened in early afternoon and by evening a distant storm had swelled around him into a blinding tempest. He managed to navigate his way back to his camp where he remained until the storm passed five days later. He lay at night and listened to the fierce wind slapping the sides of his tent and smiled at the thought of Ania feeding her kindling to the insatiable fire, or burying herself in the warmth of their bed, nothing but her pink nose poking out from the mountain of quilts.

When, on the morning following the storm, he came back after nearly two unintended weeks in the wild with the rump, shank, flank, and loin of a cow elk slung over the back of the big lumbering buttermilk dun, a quiet stillness consumed the cabin. Snowdrifts along the southern and eastward walls were much higher than he had seen before and the eerie quiet closed in on him and gave him a sensation such as vertigo. He called out for her only to be answered by his own echo. The cabin showed no signs of struggle or disarray; the kindling box next to the fireplace stood empty, the fire burned down to cold white ash.

Ethom searched the woods around the cabin until nightfall but found no trace of her. On two separate occasions, in anger from the cold, Ania had said to him that she would make her way back to Spokane, wait for him to come to his senses and join her back in the flat. He had often feared this in the cold nights when the chill got to the bones, deep in the marrow where the fire could not find it. A nagging fear that he would return to the cabin to find her gone plagued him. He knew deep down that Ania was not made for this life. She was small-framed and fragile and faired well among the comforts of the warm two-room flat. He felt shame in the selfishness of having brought her here. In the morning he saddled the dun mare and road the trail to the Pend Oreille in hopes of finding her there, still awaiting passage on a ferry that would take her up river to where she might then make her way back to Spokane. The trail showed no signs of having been traveled, but it was heavy with the deluge of new fallen snow from the storm and Ethom continued on until he reached the river. He searched the small groups that inhabited the banks, producing a picture of her and inquiring as to whether she had been seen boarding a ferry in the last many days. He realized that the photograph, the one he had cherished of her, the only one he owned, had been taken long before they had entered the mountains. Ethom stared into the face of Ania and knew that the harshness of the wild had taken a toll on the once youthful and smiling face, and the eyes that stared back at him from the worn and tattered paper. Had anyone seen her on the banks of the river, they would not have recognized her as the beautiful girl in the photograph.

Day ran into day, and when Ethom was made aware that she would not return he resigned himself to what he must do. He would travel to Spokane and find her there. He would take employment again in the Tomes Mercantile, as he felt sure that Mr. Tomes would welcome his return, having nearly broken down and pleaded with Ethom to stay. If the flat had been rented he would find another. The Great Fire had ignited a boom in the town and reparations had restored the damage much faster than had been expected, and with the renewed growth, and the railroads, came a need for housing. Flats were in ample supply. He knew that she knew he would come. And he knew she would wait for him.

When all was ready, Ethom turned back to the cabin. Smoke from the smoldering coals of his last fire still plumed from the chimney and drifted out toward him as he stood in the snow and preserved the scene through the lens in his mind. This was the home he had so longed for and so longed to share with her. Seeing it now empty and from a distance he felt as though he were viewing a two-dimensional painting. An advertisement of empty happiness. A portrait of what he once imagined could be, but realized never would. Without her it was only stacks of pine and stone. He felt contentment knowing that he had touched it. Felt the realization of his dream and overcame the primal need to be driven by it. The memory would now be enough to sustain him through the endless stocking of shelves. The throngs of dutiful wives scratching and gnawing their way through the mercantile like mice, engaged in mindless chitchat over sundries. The long sleepless nights of the city streets buzzing like a thousand flies below his window. The hollow pursuits of social standing, and the vain meaningless grasp at opulence for opulence's sake alone. His sacrifice had at that moment matured him into the realms of reliable men. Men who put aside themselves and their dreams to dream the dreams of the ones they love. Men who come to at least a vague understanding that there are things that pull at them harder than the things they wish for. A drawing deep in the spirit that almost goes unnoticed and borders on instinct. He took a large plug of tobacco from his pocket and cut a thick wedge and pushed it into his cheek tight against his jaw, turned up the trail in the direction of town and disappeared into the dense line of alder, black walnut, birch, and black jack pine; the big buttermilk dun on a lead line plodding along behind.

In late February small droplets of water began to form at the tips of the icicles that decorated the little cabin. Gradually they began to drop and fall into the snowdrift packed along the outer cabin wall. Day after day the icicles became smaller and the snowdrift, once protected by the shade of the eave, began to relent, emaciating in the oncoming warmth of spring.

After a time, Ania began slowly to emerge from the snow, lying peacefully on her side thirty-odd yards from the cabin door. Frozen. Preserved as though she had laid down that very morning to rest. An empty kerosene lantern at her side, the small kindling hatchet clutched in her icy hand, heading in the opposite direction of her neatly stacked woodpile.

ABOUT THE AUTHOR

Stacy Dean Campbell is a novelist whose work focuses on voice, restraint, and the interior lives of ordinary people. His fiction is marked by spare, lyrical prose and unflinching emotional honesty and often unfolds in small towns and overlooked spaces, tracing the inner lives of people navigating loss, endurance, and the slow passage of time. He lives in Tennessee. *Hope is a Hard Thing* is his first story collection.

922 Main Street
Suite C#169
Nashville, TN 37206